MW00988014

WHITE RIVER WOLVES

JANIE'S SALVATION

DAWN SULLIVAN

All rights reserved. No part of this publication may be reproduced, stored in a retrieval system, or transmitted in any form or by means mechanical, electronic, photocopying, recording or otherwise without prior permission from the author. This is a work of fiction. Names, characters, places and events are fictitious in every regard. Any similarities to actual events or persons, living or dead are purely coincidental. Any trademarks, service marks, product names or featured names are assumed to be the property of their respective owners and are used only for reference. There is no implied endorsement of any of these terms are used. Except for review purposes, the reproduction of this book in whole or in part, mechanically or electronically, constitutes a copyright violation. Published in the United States of America in June 2017; Copyright 2017 by Dawn Sullivan. The right of the Author's Name to be identified as the Author of the Work has been asserted by them in accordance with The Copyright, Designs and Patent Act of 1988.

Published by Dawn Sullivan

Cover Design: Dana Leah with Designs by Dana

Copyright 2017 © Author Dawn Sullivan

Language: English

For my family and friends. Your support means the world to me. Thank you.

Janie ran swiftly through the forest, constantly looking over her shoulder, wishing she had the ability to shift so that she could move even faster. Unfortunately, she was a latent wolf shifter and had never been able to take her animal form, even though she could feel the wolf's spirit within her. She was always there, a comforting presence in Janie's somewhat sad and lonely life.

Janie moved as quickly as possible, leaping over logs, barely missing random trees, all of the time praying that she would not be caught by the men who were after her. She had no idea who they were. All she knew was that she could not allow herself to be captured by them. Since she shared her soul with her wolf, Janie had the wolf's instincts, and those instincts were on high alert right now. They were telling her to get the hell out of there, because if the people that were chasing her managed to close the distance between them, there was a very good chance that she was going to die.

Glancing back to see if her pursuers were gaining on her, Janie lost her balance and tripped over the root of a tree, a soft *cry escaping as she fell to her knees on the hard, earth-packed ground. She scrambled forward frantically on all fours, fighting to rise and take off again, but they were on her before she could. One man grabbed her from behind, rolling her roughly over onto her back as she screamed loudly, kicking out at him. Laughing at her when she managed to connect with his shin, he said, "Keep it up, she-wolf. That's the way I like my bitches. Scared as hell."*

Clenching her hand tightly into a small fist, Janie pulled back her arm and let it fly, satisfaction filling her at the sound of bone breaking when it connected with his nose. Bringing her knee up, she slammed it into the asshole's balls, as she raked her nails across his face. The man cursed loudly, letting go of her to grab his dick. Janie shoved him hard, pushing him off of her, and struggled to her feet to run again.

"Do it," a low, deadly voice said quietly. "Trust me, you won't get far." Looking behind her, she saw a man with a long scar running from his temple to his chin, pointing a gun at her, his lips turned up into a vicious grin. Janie stopped in her tracks, trembling as she stared down the barrel of the revolver. She didn't want to die, but maybe it would be better than whatever these men were going to do to her. Before she could make up her mind, a third guy appeared out of nowhere. Grabbing her wrists, he slapped on a pair of thick handcuffs, before shoving her roughly back in the direction she'd just come from.

She couldn't let them take her. She knew if she did, she might not survive. Swinging around, she hit her assailant in the side of the head with her fists, catching him by surprise. Before she could make her next move, she felt a slight sting in the side of her neck, and then she was falling slowly to the ground, unable to move. Her eyes began to drift shut, and the last thing she heard before she lost consciousness was, "The General wants you, girl. And what the General wants, the General gets."

Janie woke up in a cold sweat, her hands clutching her comforter tightly. The dream was back, not that it had ever really left. It had been over two years since she was taken by the General's men, but no matter how hard she tried, she still couldn't get what happened to her out of her head. She had gone through hell and back when she was held captive by that bastard. She was still in hell. She might have been rescued by RARE last April, but the panic and terror of her captivity was still in the forefront of her mind. She lived her life in fear, terrified that the General and his soldiers would find her and drag her back to the horror she had barely managed to escape. She could not let that happen. She had a daughter who needed her, and there was no way they were getting Alayna. That little girl was her life. She would die before she let those bastards touch her.

Snuggling down into her covers, Janie wrapped her arms tightly around her pillow as she thought about her past. She used to be strong and independent, able to take care of herself. Now she was quiet and timid, just a shadow of the person she was before her life was turned upside down. Her hell began the day she became no one to her family and friends.

Janie came home from work one day to find that her alpha had decided to kick her out of the pack because she was a latent wolf. She couldn't shift, which to him meant she was defective, and he only wanted pure bloodlines in his pack. Alpha Byron Reed was afraid that if Janie mated with one of his wolves, their children would not be able to shift, which meant they would be defective as well. Janie had lived with his negative opinions and snide comments all of her life, choosing to ignore them as best she could. Life was hard because the rest of the wolves followed his lead, keeping their distance from her. The only one who hadn't, was her sister, Silver.

To Janie's shock, her parents had agreed with the alpha's decision, giving him their full support. Silver was the only one who fought for her to stay, but since she was only twenty-one at the time, and female, there wasn't much she could do. Janie was cast out on her own, only allowed to take the clothes on her back and the shoes on her feet. Luckily, the Alpha hadn't known about the money she had scrounged and saved in case something like this were to happen. She'd hid the money in a small metal box stuck inside the crevice of a tree on the outskirts of the village, and she was able to retrieve it when she left.

Janie had nowhere to go. She had no other family, and no friends in the small town she grew up in. Silver was her best friend...her only friend. She was also the only one willing to defy the alpha for her, but Janie loved her too much to allow her to do it.

After telling her devastated sister goodbye, Janie went into the nearest city and took a bus to a small town outside of San Diego, California, where she hoped to find a local wolf pack that would allow her to join them. As much as she did not want to leave the only place she had ever known, there was nothing for her there anymore.

Getting on that bus had been the worst decision Janie ever made. When she got to California, she was too afraid to contact the pack in San Diego to ask them to take her in. Instead, she ended up with a waitressing job in a rundown diner, and a small efficiency apartment that she shared with several cockroaches. She was miserable, but with nowhere else to turn, she managed the best she could.

One night while Janie was working, three huge, terrifying men came into the diner. She watched them out of the corner of her eye, as they walked past several empty tables, until they finally stopped in her section. One of them glanced in her direction, before pulling out a chair and sitting down, looking as if he deliberately sat at one of her tables. She could feel all three of their gazes on her, raking over her body, even though she refused to lift her eyes from her notepad while taking their orders. She didn't know who they were, but the feeling of trepidation running through her would not leave.

That night, when Janie left to go home, the men followed her. She ran all of the way to her apartment, slamming the door and locking it behind her. Unfortunately, the deadbolt wasn't strong enough and they managed to kick the door in, but Janie was already out the window in the living room and heading down the fire escape. One followed her, while another one ran back the way they had come. The third guy was waiting at the bottom of the fire escape when she jumped from the ladder to the pavement. Laughing, he grabbed her arm, holding her in place. "A spitfire, aren't ya?" he drawled.

"Let's go," another voice interrupted. "The General wants her." Janie had no idea at the time who the General was, and she wished she still didn't. She fought to free herself, but it was no use. One of the men, the one with the scar on his face, covered her mouth with his hand to muffle her screaming. Wrapping his arm tightly around her waist, he picked her up as if she weighed nothing and carried her to a car that was parked in the alley behind her apartments. After shoving her into the back seat, he followed her in and slammed the door shut behind them.

They'd driven for a couple of hours before finally stopping at a small gas station. Janie remembered having no idea where they were, but it did not stop her from trying to escape. She'd gotten one of them to take her to the bathroom, and while he waited just outside the door, she squeezed through a small window above the sink and snuck out, running swiftly through the forest of trees in the back of the building. Unfortunately, they figured out quickly what happened and it did not take them long to catch up with her. She never really had a chance.

What happened after that was so horrible, Janie hated to think about it. She became a test subject in the General's breading program. He paired her with Brent, a vile, nasty man who thought it was just as fun to beat her as it was to take her against her will. She had lived for the times when the General sent him out on missions, because for just a little while, she did not have to feel the slimy bastard's fingers on her skin. After a year and a half, Brent finally succeeded in getting her pregnant, and shortly after that she was moved to a new facility. The only good thing about being transferred was that she was finally away from Brent.

Janie was held at the facility for months with a young bear cub, two little wolf pups, and Flame, another pregnant woman. During that time, she had horrible things done to her that she refused to talk about to anyone. She kept it all locked up, hidden deep inside, praying the day would come when it would all just disappear and she could move on with her life.

After Janie and Flame were rescued, they were brought to the White River Wolves compound. Janie was shocked when the alpha, Chase Montgomery, offered her not only a place to stay, but also his protection, even after he found out she was a latent wolf. She'd accepted his generosity, knowing she had nowhere else to go, and became a part of his pack. Janie and Flame now shared a two-bedroom apartment in the compound, but she hardly ever saw the other woman. Flame had become a member of RARE, and was gone most of the time, either training to take down the General or out of town on special missions. She was driven by revenge after the death of her child.

Janie was not interested in revenge. She wanted to forget about the past and concentrate on the present and future. That was difficult to do though, when she had no idea if the General had given up on her, or if he was just waiting for the right time to kidnap her and her daughter. The son-of-a-bitch was not going to get her baby. She would fight to the death for her little girl. She may live in fear most of the time after everything she'd been through, scared of what could happen if the General was looking for her, but that didn't mean she was broken.

Sighing, Janie glanced at the clock. It was early morning, but she felt drained after her nightmare. If she was lucky, she would be able to get another couple of hours of sleep in. Pulling the blankets up to her neck, Janie closed her eyes and inhaled deeply, taking in the delicious smell outside her bedroom window. It had been there almost every night since she moved into the apartment. At first, she'd had no idea what it was. If she hadn't run into *him* on accident that day so long ago, she probably still wouldn't know. Xavier Andrews, one of the enforcers for the pack...her mate. She knew it, and her wolf knew it. She might not be able to shift, but she still had her wolf, and they both immediately recognized the other half of their soul.

After that day, Xavier kept his distance from her. He was kind, always smiling gently in her direction if they crossed paths, but never directly approaching her. At first Janie thought that maybe he didn't want her after what the General's men did to her. Maybe he thought she was damaged goods, and because of that, he could not accept her. It took her another couple of months to realize that if he didn't want her, he would not stand guard below her window, protecting both her and Alayna while they slept. He wasn't denying her. He was giving her time, time she desperately needed to heal, before he claimed her.

Now, Janie made sure that she left the window cracked open slightly at night so that she could fall asleep to his scent, but it was always fading away when she woke in the morning. It was comforting and soothing knowing Xavier was near, and it bothered her on the nights when he was gone. She assumed he was working those nights, but knowing that he wasn't outside watching over her caused the fear and loneliness to crowd in.

Janie smiled, snuggling deeper into her comforter. Tonight was one of her lucky nights. Knowing Xavier was there made the memories of her nightmare begin to fade away. Slowly, Janie drifted back to sleep, her mate's scent tickling her nose, seeping into her pores, making her feel safe and protected.

2

"Where the hell have you been?" Aiden demanded. "We are supposed to be at a meeting with the alpha in ten minutes. I'm not getting my ass chewed because you can't tell time."

Xavier glared at Aiden, flipping him off as he stalked passed him to get to his bedroom. "I was busy," he muttered, slamming the door shut in his brother's stunned face.

"Dammit, X. I'm going without you," he threatened.

Xavier ignored him as he stripped out of the shorts he was wearing and quickly pulled on a pair of jeans and a tee-shirt. After sliding his feet into a pair of boots, he slipped a knife into a hidden holster in his right one, then went to get his Glock. He was exhausted, worried about his mate, and pissed because he knew he was about to be sent away on another assignment. He was tired of being gone all of the time. He wanted to be home. He wanted time to try and get to know the woman who was supposed to be his for the rest of their lives, even if she didn't realize it. He wanted to be there to protect her and her daughter, instead of relying on others to do it. He wanted to be a father to little Laynie. He wanted so much, but it was all just out of reach.

With a snarl, Xavier swung around and put his fist through the wall, his fangs throbbing as they threatened to punch through his gums. He just wanted his fucking mate. It was so hard to see her, breathe in her scent, and not be able to talk to her or hold her close. He made sure to keep his distance so that he didn't scare her. After everything she'd been through, he knew she had to be terrified of anything with a dick. And that just made him even more angry.

The door opened, and Aiden stepped quietly into the room. "Xavier."

"I sleep outside her window in my wolf form, Aiden," Xavier ground out. "Every night that we are home, that is where I sleep. I can't help it. I can't stay away. I have to be near her, and it's the only way I can get close." Walking over to a chair in the corner of the room, Xavier sat down, placing his elbows on his knees and lowering his head. Shoving his fingers into his long, brown hair, he rasped, "Last night she had a nightmare. She woke up screaming and there wasn't a damn thing I could do about it. She has them a couple times a week. It's better now. It used to be every night."

He felt his brother cross the room to stand beside him, and then Aiden rested a comforting hand on his shoulder. "I'm sorry, man. I know this is hard on you. It's been a year. Maybe she will be ready to accept you now. You will never know unless you try."

Xavier stiffened, slowly raising his gaze to meet

Aiden's. "And if she rejects me? You know what those bastards did to her, Aiden. There is a good chance she might never be able to accept me. What the hell am I going to do then?"

Aiden squeezed his shoulder, before taking a step back. "Then you fight like hell for her, little brother. I've never known you to give up before."

Xavier's eyes hardened, and he gritted his teeth. Giving his brother a quick nod, he rose and stalked to the door. "You're right. She's my mate. I would do anything for her. Hell, I will wait forever if I have to."

"Right now I am more worried about what the alpha and his mate are going to do to us since we are about to be late," Aiden teased, following him out the door of their apartment and down the stairs.

Xavier reached up and pulled his hair back, tying it at the nape of his neck. "Yeah," was all he said, quickly crossing the street to the office building and taking the front stairs two at a time. He had never been late to a meeting before, and he knew he needed to get his head out of his ass, but none of it seemed to matter like it used to. There was only one thing that mattered, and she was in the apartment complex across from his, probably still sleeping since it was the ass crack of dawn.

Aiden knocked on Chase's door when they reached the alpha's office, opening it after they were told to enter. Chase sat behind his large desk talking on the phone. His mate, Angel, stood behind him, one hand resting lightly on his shoulder. They'd just recently had their mating ceremony, which gave Xavier hope that someday he would have his own. Chase had also waited over a year for Angel to accept the mate bond. Unfortunately the circumstances were very different. Angel thought she was doing what was best for her children at the time, whereas Janie had been violated in ways no woman should ever be put through. Just the thought of it had Xavier fighting to control his wolf, who wanted out to hunt down and kill anyone and everyone who had hurt his sweet mate.

Leaning casually against the wall beside the door, Xavier tapped his fingertips impatiently against his thigh as he waited for Chase to finish the call he was on. A low growl of frustration slipped out before he could contain it. Today was worse than normal. The desire to be with Janie, to slay all of her demons and make her his, was clawing at his insides. Hell, maybe it would be best if Chase did send him on a mission. Who knew what he was capable of in the state he was in right now. He would never hurt his mate, but he did not want to push her into anything she wasn't ready for, either.

"Am I keeping you from something, Xavier?" Chase asked quietly, raising his eyebrows in question after he ended his call.

Knowing he was being an ass, Xavier bared his neck in submission, and as an apology. "No, Alpha." He kept it short and sweet. The sooner this conversation was over, the better.

Chase leaned back in his chair, his eyes on Xavier, "Anything you want to talk about, son?"

Stiffening, Xavier focused on a spot just above Chase's shoulder. No one had called him son in the past twenty years, and that was the way he wanted to keep it. When Xavier and Aiden were just seven years old, their father became a traitor to the White River Wolf pack. He had been jealous of Chase's father, wanting the power and prestige the alpha title gave the other man. Because of this, he divulged information about the White River wolves to a rival pack that was trying to take over the Montgomery's territory. In doing so, he caused the death of several innocent men and women, including Xavier and Aiden's mother, and Chase's parents. When Chase became Alpha, his first order was to have Xavier's father killed. Xavier and Aiden were placed with their aunt to be raised. Aunt Sadie loved them unconditionally, and treated them like her own until she passed away just five years ago.

Unfortunately, the twins had to live with knowing their father was not only a traitor, but also a murderer. Xavier could handle it most of the time, but no one called him son. He'd had one father, and did not want or need another one.

"No, Sir," he responded, once again keeping his answer short. He did not want to disrespect his alpha, and in his current mood he knew he would if he said too much.

Sighing deeply, Chase reached up and settled a hand over Angel's. "I have had reports of suspicious activity on the northern region of our property. To make sure that the compound is not infiltrated again, I have decided to set up a patrol unit on all of the outer regions of our land for the next month or two. I sent enforcers to the north, west, and east edges of our property lines and need the two of you to go to the southern edge. You will be gone for two weeks, so plan accordingly."

Xavier clenched his hands tightly into fists as he listened to Chase. It was a direct order, one which he had to obey. And in truth, a part of him wanted to go if whatever was out there was a threat to his mate and her child.

He just hated leaving her alone for so long, especially at night. They were the hardest for his Janie.

Lowering his head, Xavier sucked in a deep breath, trying to get control of his emotions. He could feel his nails lengthening into claws, and digging into his palms. He knew his eyes had gone wolf and his fangs had dropped at the thought of a threat so close to Janie and Alayna. It will only be for a couple of weeks, Xavier told himself. Just fourteen days. He would make sure there were no enemies trying to sneak into the compound from the southern border, and then he would come back home to his mate and child.

"You have your orders," Chase told them. "I will send someone out to relieve you in two weeks."

"Yes, Sir," Aiden responded. "We will leave within the hour." Reaching over, Aiden grasped Xavier's arm and tugged, trying to pull him out of the room, but Xavier didn't budge.

"X," he growled softly, "let's go."

Eyes narrowing on Xavier, Chase rose and walked around the desk, stalking slowly towards him. "Xavier, are you ready to talk yet, son?"

"I'm not your fucking son," Xavier growled, raising his head to glare at Chase before turning to walk out the door.

"Xavier," Angel called out softly, making him pause and glance back, even though he wanted nothing more than to get the hell out of there. "I promise, I will make sure your mate is safe while you are gone."

"And if you leave for a mission?" he snarled, knowing he was walking a thin line, but unable to stop himself.

"I will be going to look for Jeremiah soon," Angel told

him, "but I will leave four of my team members behind to watch over Janie."

"Flame," Xavier said immediately. "She feels comfortable with her."

"Flame will stay," Angel agreed. "Who else?"

The tension slowly began to leave him, and his claws retracted, his vision going back to normal as he replied, "I trust you to choose the other ones."

"Steele, Storm, and Bane will stay," Angel decided. "We will give them an apartment in Janie's building to use while they are here."

Xavier swallowed hard, his eyes going from Angel to Chase. "Thank you, Alpha," he managed to say, before turning and leaving the room quickly. He knew he was being rude, but he wanted to try and catch a small glimpse of his beautiful Janie before he and Aiden left. Something to hold him over for the next long, lonely couple of weeks.

"Shit," Chase said, raking his hand through his hair as he watched Aiden follow his brother out the door. "I forgot about Janie. No wonder he's pissed. Not too long ago that was me. I know how the young wolf feels."

He sighed when he felt Angel's hand slide lightly across his shoulders, then down his back and around his waist as her arms encircled him from behind. "We both know how he feels," she whispered, kissing the middle of his back. A shiver ran up his spine at the feel of her lips through the material of his shirt. "He's a good man, trying to put Janie's fears and feelings first, but I think it is about time he let her figure out what those feelings are."

Chase clasped her hands tightly in his own, bringing one up to gently kiss each knuckle individually. "Now, tell me why you are really leaving four of your teammates behind to watch over Janie when you leave tomorrow, instead of just sending one of them in Xavier's place."

Angel chuckled softly, tugging her hands out of his grasp so that she could step around in front of him. Her light blue eyes sparkled with humor as she admitted, "They were staying behind anyway, all except Flame. I can't take the entire team with me anymore. My plane isn't big enough. I need to buy a new one."

"And you didn't send one of them with Aiden because?"

A devilish grin on her lips, his mate responded, "Like I said, it's time for Janie to decide what she wants. Xavier is almost to his breaking point. I think these two weeks away from her will be just enough to get him there."

A short burst of laughter left him, and Chase shook his head in wonder. "You never cease to amaze me, woman. Let's hope you aren't poking the beast."

Angel shrugged. "Maybe it's a beast that needs poking."

3

Janie sat on one of the benches in front of the hospital, her daughter sleeping in the stroller next to her. She looked lonely, and so damn sad. Xavier wanted nothing more than to go over and comfort her, but he didn't think she would welcome him.

His mate was the most beautiful woman Xavier had ever laid eyes on, with her long blonde hair and big hazel eyes. Janie was tiny, and had curves in all the right places. She seemed so innocent and fragile, but he knew there was a hidden strength to her. At first he'd been afraid the bastards had broken her, but after Laynie was born, that strength and determination to love and protect her daughter above all else had shone through . No, she wasn't broken, but he didn't know if she would ever be able to fully move on after everything she had gone through.

"Go talk to her, man," Aiden encouraged, giving him a light shove. "Just go say hello or something."

Xavier shook his head. He didn't ever want to upset or scare Janie, and he was afraid if she found out about him right now, she would run. "I can't, Aiden. She needs time to heal."

"Go, X," Aiden insisted. "She's had a year. I think that's enough time."

"You don't know that," Xavier said quietly. "It may never be enough time." Just then, Janie looked up with a lost expression on her face, tears in her eyes. One escaped, slowly slipping down her cheek. Xavier couldn't fight the pull to close the distance between them any longer. "Aiden..."

"She needs you right now, Xavier. Go to her. I promise, I will be right behind you, little brother."

JANIE SHIVERED, a slight chill creeping into her bones as she struggled to gain control of her emotions. She'd woken up that morning, a sense of urgency pushing at her. She had no idea why, and it terrified her. There was just this feeling that something was going to happen, and there was nothing she could do to stop it. What was it? Was her daughter in danger? Should she leave the White River Wolves compound and go on the run to keep her safe? She knew the alpha had sworn to protect both her and Alayna when she became a part of his pack, but what if he couldn't?

Janie was so lost in thought, that she didn't see the man standing in front of her until he knelt before her and whispered her name. Letting out a soft gasp of surprise, she started to move away, but then stopped when her gaze met his. Gentle, brown eyes stared back at her in concern. Xavier. She let her gaze slowly wander over him, as she tried to get her racing heart under control.

His long, dark hair was pulled back at the nape of his neck, and shock filled her when she realized her fingers were itching to touch it. Her eyes were drawn to the slight stubble that covered his jawline, and then to his lips, where the bottom one was slightly fuller than the top. Instead of the normal terror she felt when a male got too close, a feeling of peace wove through her, making her want to lean into him and accept his comfort. She had imagined this day for so long, the time when her mate would actually talk to her. Wondering if she would be able to form complete sentences, or if she would be too scared to respond. What she was finding out, was that even though he was just a few inches from her, she wasn't afraid at all.

"What's wrong, sweetheart?" he asked gently, shifting so that one knee was on the ground, while the other was raised with his arm resting casually on it. A gentle breeze chose that moment to blow by, and her nostrils flared as she inhaled that same delicious, addicting smell that was outside her window nightly. Sighing, Janie gave into the uncontrollable urge to touch him, and reached out to gently cup his cheek in the palm of her hand. She shuddered slightly at the feel of his rough, day-old stubble on her skin, something she had never thought she would ever feel again racing through her. Desire. Eyes widening in shock, she pulled back and moved to stand up.

"Wait," Xavier said, gently catching her hands in his and pulling her back down on the bench. "Tell me what's wrong, Janie. I can't fix it if I don't know what's wrong."

Janie could not seem to get enough of his expressive,

heart-stopping eyes. She did not know Xavier well, but now was her chance to change that. Biting her lip, Janie stared into her mate's eyes, whispering honestly, "I don't know. I guess I'm just emotional right now. It's nothing you or anyone else can fix, I have to do it on my own."

Shaking his head, Xavier reached out slowly and gently ran a hand down her thick, blonde hair, pushing a stray piece behind her ear. "You don't ever have to do anything alone, Janie. You are a part of the pack. We are all family. We lean on one another."

Xavier seemed so gentle and kind, like no man she'd ever met before. And that smell...closing her eyes, she inhaled deeply, letting his scent fill her, feeling her wolf perk up and take notice. *Mine.* After a moment, she opened her eyes again, a small smile teasing her lips. Catching sight of a man standing behind Xavier, Janie stiffened, rising and reaching for Alayna's stroller.

"It's okay, he's not going to hurt you. I'm Xavier and this is my brother, Aiden." Gently, Xavier once again guided her back down on the bench before standing up and backing away a few steps. Janie trembled, whimpering softly at the loss of his nearness.

"We are twins, obviously," Aiden teased, keeping his distance. "Just remember that I'm the better looking one and you won't ever get us confused."

Raising a delicate eyebrow, Janie surprised herself when a grin slipped free and she replied, "How could I get you confused? You smell nothing alike. Xavier smells so much better." Her eyes widened as she slammed her hand over her mouth, her cheeks reddening in embarrassment, when both men burst out laughing.

"I'm sure he does to you," Aiden said, still chuckling.

"I'm going to go pack. I'll see you at the apartment in a few minutes, X. We need to leave soon." With a cocky grin toward Janie, and a salute to Xavier, Aiden left them. Janie watched him go with a small smile on her face, until what he had said registered. He must know Xavier was her mate. She wondered who else knew. Shame filled her at the thought of how long she had been trying to deny the mate bond. She'd taken advantage of Xavier, needing him near, but not accepting him in front of his family and friends. Did they all know? And then the second thing he said sank in. They were leaving.

"May I sit with you?" Xavier asked, watching her closely as he waited for her reply. She nodded slowly, needing him near her, as she moved over on the bench closer to her daughter. When he sat beside her, keeping a small distance between them, she breathed in his scent again, sighing appreciatively. It was so addictive. She swore she could live on his scent alone.

"It's early to be out," Xavier remarked, nodding to Alayna. "Why aren't you both still in bed?"

Janie reached over and ran a finger over the soft skin of her daughter's cheek, before whispering, "I woke early and needed to get out of the apartment." She didn't tell him that without him outside her window, she was unable to get back to sleep again the second time she woke from a bad dream. "Alayna was still sleeping, and I didn't want to leave her alone, so I decided to put her in her stroller and go for a walk."

"And you ended up here?"

Janie shrugged. A part of her had wondered why she'd chosen to stop at the hospital, too, but deep down she knew. "I like it here," was all she said. She couldn't tell him the full truth. The hospital was the one place she could go, and know that someone would always be there for her if she needed them. Doc Josie was her rock, the person she leaned on the most in the compound. She'd come here that morning because she was debating on talking to the doctor about this urgent feeling she was having, making her suspect that something was wrong. She didn't know where else to go.

"So, tell me, why are you so upset, sweetheart?" Xavier asked softly. Janie bit her lower lip, wanting to confide in him. When he called her sweetheart like that, the way the endearment rolled across his tongue, it made her feel special. She wanted to tell him everything and let him fix it, like he said he wanted to earlier. Unfortunately, it was not anything he could just fix.

"I honestly don't know what it is," Janie finally confessed, looking down at her hands that were now clasped tightly in her lap. When had she become such a pitiful, pathetic version of the person she used to be? Until she was kicked out of her old pack, she had been a strong, confident woman. Even after she was forced to leave the only home she had ever known, she was able to take care of herself. She had been proud of the person she was, and even though it was hard living without a pack, she survived. Until the General's men. "It's nothing," she lied.

Xavier was quiet for a moment before he replied, "Maybe you would feel more comfortable talking to someone else?"

Janie heard the hurt in his voice, and glanced over at him. The pain in his eyes was quickly masked when they met hers, and she found herself reaching out involuntarily to touch his arm briefly before pulling back and bowing her head. "I'm sorry," she whispered.

"You have nothing to be sorry for," he told her, raising his hand hesitantly, before letting it fall back to the bench between them. "I need to get going," he said quietly.

"Where?" Janie asked, before she could stop herself. Biting her bottom lip, she worried it through her teeth as she waited for his response. When a low growl filled the air, her head snapped up, and her breath caught in her throat at the heated look in his eyes as he stared at her mouth. "Xavier?" she breathed, uncertainty in her voice. She should be terrified right now, but she wasn't. She was so many things, but scared definitely was not on the list.

Xavier stood quickly, putting distance between them. "Aiden and I have to go to work." When he rested his hands on his hips, Janie's gaze was inadvertently drawn to the thick bulge in the front of his pants. Her heart skipped a beat, and she licked her lips nervously. "Baby, you have got to stop doing that," Xavier groaned, taking another step away from her.

"What?" she whispered in confusion, dragging her gaze from the evidence of his arousal, up to meet his now dark chocolate colored eyes. His scent had thickened, and it curled around her, seeping into her pores.

Her tongue snuck out to wet her bottom lip again, and Xavier took another step back, his eyes glued to her lips. "Fuck, I have to go."

Janie didn't want him to go. She wanted...she paused when the truth of what she really wanted sunk in. She wanted to feel his lips on hers. She wanted to see if he tasted as good as he smelled, and her wolf was in full agreement. "Xavier," his name was a plea on her lips as she rose from the bench.

"Baby." With a groan, he closed the distance between them, sliding a hand up into the hair at the nape of her neck.

Janie waited in nervous anticipation as he slowly lowered his lips to hers, giving her an out if she wanted one. She thought briefly of taking it, but then his mouth covered hers and all thoughts of fleeing were instantly gone. He was gentle with her, even though she felt the tension running through him. He slowly traced her lips with his tongue, then slipped past them when she gasped in pleasure. He tasted of mint and spice, and her body trembled as the combination consumed her. His hands gently traced down her back, pulling her close. His touch was like nothing she had ever felt before.

Tentatively, Janie touched her tongue to his, reveling in the groan that tore from his throat. He let her have control, and she deepened the kiss, slipping past his lips and into his mouth. Her breath caught when his fang nicked her tongue, and she froze. *Mine!* The word echoed around in her mind, and she pulled back to look in his eyes, eyes that were churning darkly with emotion.

"Xavier," she breathed, touching her lips with her fingertips. Before he could respond, Alayna let out a loud cry. Quickly stepping back, Janie turned and rushed over to where her daughter was now sitting up in her stroller, reaching out to her with tears in her eyes. "It's okay, sweet girl," she murmured, "mommy's here."

When she turned back around with Alayna in her arms, Xavier cleared his throat, "I better go. Aiden will be looking for me soon."

"Will you be gone long?" She sounded so needy after just one kiss, but she'd felt more pleasure from his kiss than she had ever felt from another man her entire life. And not once had she thought about the soldiers who had forced themselves on her when Xavier touched her. She'd only felt him, only thought of him. And it shocked her, but she had wanted him to do more.

"A couple of weeks," he said shortly.

"Oh." Why did she suddenly feel as if her world had dropped out from under her? It wasn't as if he hadn't left the compound for days before.

Xavier walked slowly over to her, smiling down at Alayna. "Hey there, Laynie girl. How are you?"

Alayna looked at him suspiciously, then ducked her head, hiding in Janie's shoulder. When Xavier laughed, she peeked back at him, a giggle escaping. Patting Janie's cheek, she said, "Mama!"

Xavier grinned, reaching out to tug gently on a stray strand of her hair. "I have to go. Take care of your mama for me while I'm gone, princess."

"Be safe," Janie whispered.

"Always."

Xavier leaned in and lightly nuzzled her cheek the way she'd seen many wolves do to their loved ones in the past. Closing her eyes, she felt a shudder run through her body as she whispered, "Goodbye, Xavier."

"For now," he replied, placing a soft kiss on her cheek.

Was it just for now? Janie wondered as she watched him walk away. Would she still be here when he came back? The sense of urgency that had seemed to leave when Xavier was near, was back in full force.

4

They were only two days into their mission, and Xavier was already going crazy. He had been hard as a fucking rock since Janie's lips touched his, the need to claim her driving him insane. What the hell had he been thinking kissing her like that? The problem was, he hadn't been thinking at all. Not with the right head anyway. If he had, he never would have done it. Sitting on a log close to the fire he'd built just the hour before, Xavier cursed in frustration.

"Could you be any louder, X?" Aiden asked sarcastically, as he tossed more wood on the slowly burning embers. "I don't think they heard you in the next county over."

Baring his teeth at his brother, Xavier stood and started pacing back and forth, raking his fingers through his hair. "What the hell are we doing here, Aiden?"

"Our jobs," Aiden responded calmly.

"There's no one out here," Xavier growled in frustration, irritated that he was so far away from the one person he should be with right now. "No one except for us, freezing our balls off."

"Xavier, sit down."

Xavier turned to glare at his brother, "If I wanted to sit down, I would have fucking stayed where I was."

"Sit your ass down, before I sit you down," Aiden growled, his voice low and commanding.

Stiffening, his jaw set, Xavier stalked back over to the log and sat. If anyone else would have talked to him like that, he would have told them to go screw themselves, but not Aiden. Every day since that horrible night when their mother was killed, along with so many others, it had been him and Aiden against the world. They both felt as though they were unworthy of the White River Wolves' loyalty after what their father had done, even though not one member of the pack ever blamed them personally, and they fought hard to prove that they deserved it. No matter what, they always had each other's backs.

"Now," Aiden said quietly, sitting down beside him, "tell me what's going on. Is it Janie?" Xavier shrugged, looking into the fire. Of course, it was Janie. It was always Janie. "Talk to me, X."

Xavier sighed, rubbing a hand over his tired eyes and down his face. "I kissed her, man. I fucking kissed her, and I shouldn't have."

They sat in silence for a moment before Aiden asked, "And?"

"And what?" Xavier snapped back. "Isn't that enough? The woman has been through hell, and instead of giving her the time she needs to heal, I forced myself on her."

Aiden's eyes narrowed, and he growled, "Are you telling me she told you to stop, and you didn't?"

Xavier paused, "Well, no."

"She didn't tell you to stop? Didn't push you away?"

"No," Xavier said, thinking back, "she…"

"She what, Xavier?" Aiden demanded. "You either forced yourself on her, or you didn't. But I will tell you right now, little brother, you better be prepared to get your ass kicked if you did."

Xavier looked over at Aiden, his brother's eyes glowing a bright yellow hue in the dark. "She kissed me back," he whispered.

Aiden watched him closely, "Was she scared? Did you scent that anything was off?"

Xavier thought hard before shaking his head. "No, she wasn't afraid," he finally said.

A slow grin crossed Aiden's lips as he asked, "So, if she wasn't scared, then what was she?"

Xavier's heartbeat accelerated, his dick becoming even harder if that was possible, as he remembered how Janie had taken over the kiss. There wasn't an ounce of fear in her at the time. There was only pure lust. "Fuck," Xavier snarled, shoving his hands through his hair.

Aiden clapped him on the shoulder, squeezing tightly, "I think it's about time you claimed your mate, X. Sounds to me like she's ready."

Was his brother right? Was Janie ready? Xavier's body heated at the thought, as excitement began to fill him. Maybe it was time to claim his mate.

Suddenly the wind shifted, and Xavier smelled the man at the same time he heard the loud click as a bullet left the gun chamber. "Aiden!" He dove for his brother, slamming into him hard and taking him to the ground as he felt the first bullet pierce the skin of his left arm. After they hit the ground, a second entered his back. Hell, no. This was not happening. He'd just been shot the month before, and had almost died. He had no desire to go through that again.

Aiden tried to push Xavier off of him, but the gun cracked loudly, the noise echoing in the quiet night, as another bullet hit Xavier in one of his legs. "Don't move," he whispered to his brother. "The stupid bastard is coming to us. Let him."

Aiden stilled, and Xavier barely heard him breathe, "He's a dead mother-fucker."

"So, that bitch Janie is your mate, huh, mongrel? That's too bad, because we have come to take her home."

Home? A low growl began to build in Xavier's throat. Janie *was* home, and no one was taking her anywhere. He felt Aiden shift ever so slightly, and knew he was reaching for one of his knives.

"She escaped last year, and even though the General doesn't seem to give a shit about her anymore, my buddy Brent does. We are going to keep her somewhere neither you nor the General can find her, so that Brent can have her whenever he wants. You can keep her brat, though. Brent doesn't want it, even if it is his kid." The man laughed, moving even closer to them. "Of course, you would have to get to your village in time to save her. Brent should be there soon, and he plans on getting rid of her. He wants Janie's undivided attention."

Pure, raw anger filled Xavier. Alayna wasn't Brent's child. She was *his*! And no one was touching her or Janie. "Kill him," he growled, using all of his strength to push himself off of his brother, hissing in pain when Aiden shoved him hard to help.

Xavier watched through bleary eyes as the knife left Aiden's hand, embedding itself deeply in the bastard's throat. The man stared at him in shock, dropping his gun to the ground, and grasping at the handle to try and pull it out. But it was too late. Staggering forward, he fell to his knees, then on his side, his eyes wide open in death. His buddy, who appeared out of nowhere to help him, didn't stand a chance. Aiden was on him in an instant, and he was gone with a knife through his heart.

"Hurry up, Aiden," Xavier rasped, fighting to stay awake. "Call Chase and warn him, and then get these fucking bullets out of me. I need to get to my family!"

He heard Aiden's voice in the distance, but couldn't make out the words. His head was swimming, pain racking his entire body. But all he could think about was Janie. His kind, gentle mate. "Aiden. Have to save her," he rasped. They couldn't have her, dammit! She was *his*! "Janie!" her name was a cry on his lips, before the darkness took him.

5

J anie stood by the crib looking down at her daughter, tears in her eyes. They were going to have to leave. She had waited too long as it was, hoping the feeling that something bad was about to happen would leave her, but it didn't. It was building daily, and getting much worse. She didn't want to go. The White River Wolves had opened their doors to her, welcoming her into their lives and making her a part of the pack. She'd never felt like she belonged anywhere before, not even with her old pack. She wanted this life for her daughter. She wanted it for herself. And then, there was Xavier.

Janie lifted her fingers to her lips, tracing them lightly, trembling when she remembered the feel of Xavier's mouth on hers. It felt so perfect, so right, when he kissed her. As if they belonged together. Which, according to fate they did, and as far as she knew, fate didn't make mistakes. If she left, she would never feel that again. But how could she stay when the feeling that danger was near kept swamping her? She had to protect her child above all else. A lone tear slid down her cheek at the thought of losing Xavier before she even really got to know him. How could she leave her mate?

"Whatever you are thinking about doing, stop right now."

Janie stiffened, turning to face Flame who stood in the open doorway. "You promised a long time ago not to invade my thoughts," she whispered, wiping the wetness from her face.

"I couldn't help it Janie," Flame said softly, stepping into the room with her. "You are broadcasting loudly. I could feel your pain and fear the moment I opened the front door."

Janie glanced back at her daughter to make sure she was still sleeping before walking past Flame, motioning for the other woman to follow her. Leaving the door slightly ajar, Janie made her way quickly to the living room, sitting down on the sofa. "Flame, I don't think I have a choice," she started.

"You always have a choice," Flame interrupted.

Running a hand through her hair in frustration, Janie snapped, "That may be true, but this time I may have to make one that I don't want to make."

"Why?" Flame asked stubbornly, arching an eyebrow.

"Because it may be the only way to keep my daughter safe," Janie growled, "and she is what's important. She's everything to me, Flame. She's all I have." As soon as the words left her mouth, Janie knew it wasn't true. It used to be, before she'd been brought to the White River Wolves compound, but it wasn't now. She was not alone anymore. She had friends, family, and Xavier.

"Janie," Flame said quietly, sitting down next to her

and clasping Janie's shaking hands in her own, "you have me."

Janie's eyes filled with tears as she lowered her head. "I know."

"You have Chase and Angel."

Janie nodded silently, tears now flowing down her cheeks. "Yes," she whispered.

Flame hesitated before murmuring, "You have so many people who care for you, Janie. Who love you."

"Xavier," Janie whispered, swallowing hard. "You are talking about him, aren't you?"

"You know about Xavier?" Flame asked in surprise.

Janie nodded, not bothering to mask the pain from her eyes when she raised them to look at her friend. "I recognized him as my mate awhile ago." She didn't tell Flame that it had been months. She was too ashamed to admit that.

Frowning in confusion, Flame asked, "But how? I don't understand."

She and Janie had never discussed what Janie was doing in the General's breeding program. Flame hadn't asked, and Janie did not volunteer the information. The only reason she knew that Flame had the ability to read minds and speak telepathically, was because she overheard the scientists at the facility they were being held at talking to one of the guards about it when Flame was first transferred there. She was warning the others to try and mask their thoughts. When Janie had come up with the courage one day to ask Flame about it, Flame had promised her that she would never intrude on her thoughts. While it seemed that she had no problem delving into the minds of their captors, she had no desire to know what everyone else in the world was thinking.

Janie sighed, gently tugging her hands from Flame's and wrapping her arms around her waist. "It's a long story," she said softly, unsure if she should admit her flaw. "I'm a latent wolf shifter," she finally murmured, once again meeting Flame's gaze.

"What does that mean exactly?"

"It means that even though I am a shifter, and I can feel my wolf's presence inside of me, I've never been able to actually shift into my animal form," Janie explained. "I was kicked out of my pack because of it. The alpha was afraid I would mate with one of his wolves and then our children would be defective too," she muttered bitterly.

"What the hell do you mean by defective?"

Janie shrugged, "To others, there is something wrong with me because I can't shift. I'm flawed."

"Bullshit," Flame snarled. When Janie's eyes widened in surprise, she went on, "There isn't a damn thing wrong with you, Janie. You are sweet, kind, and generous. You are loyal and trustworthy. You are the first to volunteer if someone here needs help. You are a good friend, and a wonderful mother. So what if you can't shift? Fuck your old alpha. You are perfect just the way you are."

Janie looked into Flame's eyes, but saw nothing but honesty in them. She felt a small smile cross her lips as she murmured, "You really feel that way, don't you?"

"Of course I do, Janie. We never see ourselves the way others do. You are held up on what your old alpha thought, but we both know Chase doesn't feel the same way, and *he* is your alpha now. You need to remember that."

"The alpha in my other pack wasn't the only one who felt that way," Janie told her quietly. "My parents did too. They supported his decision to kick me out, and so did the rest of the pack. The only one who stood up for me was my sister. She didn't want me to leave."

She could see the storm brewing in Flame's eyes, as they darkened in fury. "Well they are all a bunch of fucking idiots then," she growled. "You are better off without them."

Janie's smile grew, and her heart warmed at her friend's protectiveness. "Thank you," she whispered.

Janie could tell Flame was still pissed, but all she did was nod before saying, "Now, tell me why you were thinking about running away. If you know Xavier is your mate, then you have to know that there is nowhere you could go that he would not follow. The man loves you, Janie. He has waited a long time to claim you. He isn't going to just let you go."

"I don't want him to," Janie admitted softly. "I don't want to leave."

"Then don't," Flame said. "Trust us to help you with whatever it is that you are afraid of. Trust me."

"I do trust you," Janie promised.

"Then talk to me."

"That's just it," Janie told her, "I don't know what it is, Flame. All I know is that something is going to happen. Someone or something is coming for me and my daughter. There's danger out there. I feel it."

Flame nodded slowly, "You should always trust your instincts, Janie. I'm going to call Angel…"

Before Flame could finish, there was a loud knock on their door. "Stay here," she ordered quietly. Removing her gun from the holster at her hip, she rose and silently made her way across the living room.

"Janie, open the door!"

Flame quickly unlocked the deadbolt, yanking the door open at the alpha's order, and Chase slipped into the apartment followed by Slade and Sable. "Stay with Janie," he ordered, before he and his enforcers quickly made their way down the hall to the bedrooms.

"Alayna," Janie cried, rising from the sofa to follow.

"They will keep her safe," Flame promised, grasping her arm tightly in one hand, while holding her gun steady and ready in the other. "Let them do their job, Janie."

As much as she wanted to fight her way to her child, Janie forced herself to stand still, her entire body shaking as she waited for her alpha to return. It seemed like forever, but suddenly he was there, placing a sleepy Alayna in her arms. She was snuggled in a pink blanket, holding her favorite teddy bear close. The moment she was in Janie's arms, Alayna rested her head on her mother's shoulder. Closing her eyes, she was out again.

"Alpha," Janie whispered in fear, "what's going on?"

"A couple of my enforcers ran into one of the General's men while on patrol," Chase said, reaching out to lay a calming hand on her arm. "He was here looking for you, Janie. He said he was with a man named Brent who has come for you."

Janie clutched Alayna tightly, shaking her head in denial. "No! I won't go back there, Alpha." Looking at Flame in terror, she cried, "I knew I should have left. I won't let them have my baby!"

Immediately she felt Chase push his power in her direction, trying to reassure and soothe her as he said,

"No one is going to get to you or your pup, Janie. I'm going to get you somewhere safe, and then we are going to find Brent and the rest of his men."

"There is no place that is safe if he is here," Janie said, her gaze going to Flame. "I need a gun."

"Janie, we will take care of you," Chase vowed quietly.

"No, I refuse to be defenseless against that bastard when he shows up. I will not go back to the General, and he is not getting my daughter. Flame, please, get me a gun."

Flame left the room and was back soon with a Glock in her hand. "Are you sure?" she asked, waiting for Janie to nod before hooking a holster securely to her thigh and sliding the gun in. "Do you know how to use it?"

Janie gritted her teeth as she nodded again. "I took lessons when I was younger. I just never thought the day would come where I would have to actually use them."

"We need to go," Chase said, urging her toward the door.

"Alpha, Aiden's almost here with Xavier," Slade cut in from behind them. "Doc Josie has the operating room ready, but it sounds like Xavier is not cooperating. He is refusing treatment at this time."

Janie stopped at the door, turning quickly to look at Slade. "What's wrong with Xavier?" she demanded.

Slade froze, his gaze going to Chase and then back to her. Janie watched as his brow furrowed in confusion, before suddenly widening in understanding. "It's nothing to worry about, Janie. He's going to be just fine."

Janie heard the lie in his voice, smelled it in the air. For the first time in her life, her eyes changed, flashing a dark golden color, and her gums began to ache as a growl built deep in her chest. "What is wrong with my mate?" She accentuated each word individually, taking a step toward him as anger flowed through her. Xavier was hers, dammit. They would not keep information about him from her. As his mate, she had a right to know what was going on.

"Holy shit," Flame gasped, causing Janie to turn in her direction. "Are you sure you can't shift, Janie? Because you look awfully close to doing it right now."

Janie bared her teeth, satisfaction filling her when she felt her fangs punch through her gums. "Where is my mate?" she demanded, her body trembling with fury. How dare they keep information about Xavier from her? Suddenly, the sound of Alayna's soft whimper broke through her rage. Slowly, she loosened her hold on her daughter, closing her eyes and burying her head in the crook of Alayna's neck as she tried to get control of her emotions.

She felt Chase pushing his alpha power toward her again, and then he was next to her, running a hand gently down her hair. "Xavier is going to be fine, Janie," he promised. "Aiden said he was shot, but that he thought all major organs were missed." When she glanced up at him, still looking through her wolf's eyes, he asked gently, "How long have you known he is your mate?"

"Months," she admitted, through tightly clenched teeth. "Take me to him." When it looked as if they were going to protest, she bared her teeth and growled, "Now!"

She saw the shock in Flame's eyes, but ignored it as she turned and quickly left the apartment, Alayna still clutched tightly in her arms. Xavier was hers, and they would not keep them apart when he needed her.

"Janie, you need to think about your daughter," Flame said, catching up with her. "We have to keep her safe."

Janie didn't stop moving. "She will be safe with me." They could follow her or not, she didn't care. She was finding her mate.

"Let it go," she heard Chase say, and then he was in front of her, leading the way out of the apartment building and across the compound.

A vehicle screeched to a stop in front of the building just as they reached the hospital gardens. Janie watched as Aiden jumped out of the driver's seat and ran around to the passenger side. Opening the door, he reached in and hauled his brother out of the SUV.

Janie stared at Xavier, her eyes raking over his blood covered body. He had obviously been shot more than once. Her eyes widened at the deep growl that erupted from Xavier's throat. Her mate was there. And he was pissed.

6

Xavier snarled, grabbing hold of the truck door as he tried to pull free of Aiden's grasp. He cursed darkly when his gaze wavered, and he had to fight the urge to black out again. He was weak, light-headed from blood loss, and unable to shift to heal faster because of the bullets Aiden had refused to remove on his own.

"Dammit, X," Aiden hissed, struggling to hold him up, "stop acting like a dumbass. We need to get into the hospital and let the doc take a look at you."

"What I need to do is get to Janie before that bastard Brent finds her," Xavier growled, shaking his head to try and get rid of the dizziness he was experiencing.

"Well, you aren't going to be of any help to her this way," Aiden said, tightening his hold around Xavier's waist and turning to move toward the hospital stairs. "You need to let Chase take care of her until you can. Hell, right now you couldn't fight your way out of a paper sack."

"Fuck you, Aiden."

Aiden urged him forward. "Come on, X. Let me get

you to the operating room, and then I will go check on Janie. I will stay with her and Alayna until you can be there yourself."

Xavier knew it was a big concession for Aiden to offer to leave his side when he was hurt. Even though they were twins, Aiden had always felt that it was his duty to watch over Xavier and keep him safe. The last time he'd been shot, he almost died, and Aiden had blamed himself, barely leaving the hospital room until he was better. But he also knew Aiden understood that he was the only one Xavier trusted to take care of his mate and child while he was unable to do it himself.

Before Xavier could respond, he felt another arm wrap around his waist, and he looked down into a pair of dark golden eyes swirling with green specks. He stumbled, barely managing to catch himself as he whispered, "Janie?" He'd never seen her eyes that color before. He stiffened when his gaze narrowed on the tips of her fangs peeking out from behind her light pink lips. He had no doubt that he was looking at her wolf, one he had never seen in the year she lived with the pack. Why had she decided to show herself now? "What's wrong?" he demanded, sliding an arm over Janie's shoulder as he swayed on his feet. His eyes began to glaze over as he glanced past Janie. "Where's Laynie?"

"She's right here," Flame said, stepping forward. "She's safe. I have her."

Xavier squeezed his eyes shut tightly, sucking in a deep breath when Aiden moved his arm up and accidentally grazed the wound in his back. His sweet Janie let loose a deadly growl that shocked the hell out of him, and he wished he could see the look on her face. He'd never seen this side of her before, and even though he felt like he was going to pass out, it made him hard as hell.

"What have you done to yourself now, Xavier Andrews?" Xavier heard Doc Josie's voice, but it sounded so far off, and he could not open his eyes to respond. He groaned, trying to push back the darkness that threatened to claim him. "Shit, get him in the hospital now," the doctor ordered.

Xavier groaned in pain when Aiden slid an arm under his legs and lifted him. He felt Janie slip away from him, and he tried to protest the loss of her touch, but he couldn't seem to get the words out. He began to struggle in Aiden's arms, his only thought to get back to Janie. His mind was muddled and confused, and he could not seem to get a grasp on what was happening. All he knew was that his mate was in danger, and she needed him.

"I've got you, X," Aiden whispered, as Xavier fought weakly to get free. "Everything is going to be okay. I promise."

Bright lights swarmed overhead as his brother sat him down on what felt like cold, hard steel. "We are going to have to tie him down if he doesn't stop thrashing around like that."

"Hush," a soft, soothing voice said, as someone gently stroked a hand down his arm. "You need to calm down, Xavier. Let the doctor do her job."

Xavier bared his teeth in what he assumed was the woman's direction, but she just laughed. "I'm not afraid of the big bad wolf. I'm mated to a black panther. They are scarier than a wolf any day." A panther? Xavier shook his head in confusion. He knew who she was; mate to a member of RARE, daughter to Angel, and now recognized as the daughter of his alpha. It did not stop him though. All he could think about was protecting Janie. She was the only thing that mattered. She and little Laynie.

Xavier felt someone place a hand firmly on his shoulder and push him back against the table. He grunted as pain slammed through him, arching up to try and relieve the agony in his lower back. "Lay down, Xavier," Doc Josie demanded. "I need to see what I am dealing with here." When Xavier snarled at her, his whole body shaking as he tried to sit up, the doctor growled, "Watch yourself, pup. You will not disrespect me in my own hospital."

"Stop, Xavier." Xavier froze as Janie's voice washed over him. He breathed her scent in, immediately beginning to calm. Slowly, he let himself lay back on the cool table, moaning in pain.

"He was shot in the back, Doc." Aiden was still there. His mate and his brother. There was only one person missing.

"Laynie," he rasped, struggling to open his eyes.

"He needs your touch, Janie. He needs to know you are with him and are safe," Jade said softly.

Xavier sighed when he felt Janie's hand brush his hair back from his forehead, and then begin to stroke through the strands gently. "Laynie," he gasped again, worry for the little girl in his voice.

"She's just outside the room with Flame," Janie whispered into his ear. "She's safe, Xavier. We both are. Please, let them take care of you."

"Gun," he muttered, unable to say more.

"You saw that, did you?" Janie said, a slight teasing note in her voice. Hell yeah he had seen the Glock strapped to her thigh. Part of him had been turned on, but another part of him was mad as hell that she felt the need to carry one to protect herself. He was the one who was supposed to keep her and Laynie safe. She should not have to carry a sidearm, or any other kind of weapon.

When he didn't respond, Janie lightly ran her fingertips over his face. "It's just until they capture Brent. I need to be able to protect my daughter."

Weakly lifting his hand to capture hers, he said, "Our daughter."

He heard her gasp right before he lost the battle and succumbed to the darkness.

7

J anie leaned her head back against the chair next to the hospital bed Xavier lay in, overcome with exhaustion. It had been a long night, first in the operating room watching Doc Josie dig a bullet out of Xavier's back, and then his thigh. He'd also been nicked in the arm, but thankfully it had already closed up.

Afterwards, they moved Xavier to one of the open hospital rooms, and Janie refused to leave his side. She'd sat in the chair next to him for hours, holding her sleeping daughter close as she gazed at the man she had come to care deeply for. The man who claimed not only her, but also her child, even though Alayna wasn't his flesh and blood.

Alayna had woken up early that morning, all smiles as she sat on the bed beside Xavier and talked. Janie had no idea what the little girl was saying, but she was happy, and that was all that mattered. After eating her breakfast that one of the nursing staff brought in, she was now in Doc

Josie's office with Flame and Aiden playing with some toys the doctor kept for the children who visited.

Chase and several of his enforcers were out combing the White River Wolves' lands, looking for Brent and the rest of his friends. They had found two small campsites a couple of miles out, but nothing else as of yet. Sighing deeply, Janie reached up and rubbed at her tired eyes. She needed sleep, but there was no way she was leaving Xavier.

"Come here, sweetheart."

Xavier's rough voice broke through her thoughts, and Janie looked over to see him staring at her, his eyes full of concern. When he held out his hand, she could not stop the sob that tore from her throat. Covering her mouth with her hands, she bowed her head and let the tears she had kept bottled up all night flow freely down her cheeks. Her shoulders shook with her ragged breaths and she cried, "I was so scared, Xavier."

"Baby, please, come here and let me hold you."

It took some more coaxing, but finally Janie was out of the chair and sitting beside him on the bed. She did not resist when he lifted up the blanket and pulled her down so that she was lying next to him, her head resting on his chest. "It's okay," he whispered, covering them both with the blanket and gently rubbing a hand down her back. "I just need to shift a couple of times and I will be as good as new."

Janie slid her arm around his waist and carefully slipped one of her legs over the top of his, snuggling as close to him as she could get. "I don't want to hurt you," she whispered, raising her eyes to meet his.

"You aren't," he promised, kissing her softly on the

forehead, then the tip of her nose, and finally gently on the lips. "It was my other leg that took the bullet, but I have more aches than actual pain right now anyway."

"What the hell is that supposed to mean?" she groused. "Either it hurts or it doesn't."

Xavier laughed, cupping her cheek and wiping away the tears with his thumb. "Stop worrying so much, beautiful. I'm fine."

Janie bit her bottom lip, jumping slightly at the low growl that came from Xavier. "What did I tell you about that?" he muttered, his eyes glued to her mouth, "You can't do things like that, Janie. It makes me forget."

The tip of her tongue snuck out as Janie licked her lips nervously. "Forget what?"

"That I'm not supposed to do this right now," Xavier muttered, just before he closed the distance between them and captured her mouth with his. Janie moaned when the tip of his tongue traced her lips, and she opened up to allow access inside, which he quickly took advantage of. He groaned as he sank his fingers into her hair, cupping her head and holding her still as he tangled his tongue with hers.

Janie felt her vision blur and her gums began to ache. *Mine.* Her body trembled as she pressed closer to Xavier, the evidence of his arousal pushing against her hip. Ending the kiss, she leaned back and looked at him, licking her lips when her attention was drawn to where his shoulder met his neck. She wanted to mark him. Wanted to sink her teeth deep into his skin, and leave no doubt to anyone that he was hers. The thought made her fangs drop, and a low growl began to build in her chest.

"Fuck, Janie," Xavier rasped, sliding his hands down to

grasp her hips and pull her over so that she straddled him. His own eyes were glowing, his fangs visible as he arched up into her. "You feel so good."

"Xavier." She moaned his name loudly, sliding her hands up his bare chest, before bending over to lick at one of his nipples. Twirling her tongue around it, she sucked gently.

Janie felt a shudder run through him, as he growled, "We have to stop." When she nipped at the other nipple, he groaned, "We can't do this, baby."

Janie stiffened, raising her head to look at him. "You don't want me?" She knew that couldn't be true. His hard cock was pressed against her, and his eyes had darkened with desire. He could not hide that from her.

"Of course I want you," he rasped, gripping her hips tightly as he pushed into her again, his gaze locked on hers. "I want nothing more than to take you right now. To sink deep inside of you and claim you as my own. But you deserve so much more than a hospital bed for our first time, Janie. I want to worship you, kiss every inch of your soft, silky skin. I want to show you how much I care about you. I can't do that here."

"I don't need that," Janie protested, leaning in closer to trace her tongue down his neck, sucking the skin gently into her mouth.

Xavier groaned loudly when she ran her fangs lightly over his shoulder, "I just want to do this right," he said, his body shaking as he tried to hold back. "I don't want to scare you."

Janie raised her head to look at him, her heart filling as she realized that once again, her mate was looking out for her. After everything the General's men had put her through, he didn't want to bring back those memories, or make her relive them. Gently running a finger down the side of his face, then over his lips, she smiled at the pure love that shone in his gaze. "I'm not scared, Xavier. I could never be afraid of you. You are my mate, my soul. You would never hurt me."

"I know that," he whispered, "and on some level, you know that too. But this isn't some quick fuck, baby. This is forever. I want to spend time with you. To show you what you mean to me. You and Laynie both."

Janie relaxed against him, crossing her arms on his chest, and resting her chin on her folded hands. His hard cock pressed against her belly, and the smell of desire was thick in the air, but she was beginning to understand that even though Xavier wanted to complete their bond, he had other things on his mind too. Their future. Smiling, she murmured, "You never call her Alayna. It's always Laynie."

Xavier shrugged, a pink tinge covering his cheeks. "It's just how I think of her."

"I like it," Janie admitted, "and so will she. It will make her feel special."

"She is special," Xavier said, running a hand gently down her back. "You both are."

Janie took a deep breath, fighting back the tears that threatened to spill from her eyes. She had never felt more special than she did right now, in this man's arms. She'd never had a boyfriend before. Brent was the one who stole her virginity, something she had been saving for her mate someday. It had been brutal and painful, as was every other time he'd forced himself on her. Janie shoved the memories down viciously. That was all a part of her past now. She refused to allow it to intrude on this moment with Xavier.

"I want to do this right," Xavier went on. "I want you to get to know me, like I know you."

"Like what?" she asked, staring into his dark eyes.

A small smile teased Xavier's lips as he said, "Just the little things. Like the fact that your favorite pizza is pepperoni. Or that your favorite color is blue. And you love country music."

Janie's eyes never left his as she whispered, "Supreme, green, and rock."

"What?" he asked, frowning in confusion.

"Your favorite pizza is supreme. You ate almost a whole box of it by yourself at the Christmas party." When his eyes widened, she went on, "Your favorite color is green. You wear several different shades of it, when you aren't in your enforcer uniform. And you love rock music. It's what is always playing on your iPod when you leave your apartment to go to the gym." She blushed a little at the last part. She had just admitted to him that she looked for him when he left his apartment, praying for just a small glimpse of him.

Xavier stared at her in shock, slowly sliding a hand up to gently trace her face. "You've watched me?"

Janie nuzzled his hand with her cheek, smiling through her tears. "Every day for the past nine months," she admitted. "That's when I ran into you for the first time. When I caught your scent and knew that you were mine."

"Nine months?"

Janie nodded, lowering her head in shame. "I'm so

sorry, Xavier. It wasn't that I didn't want to be your mate. I just…"

Xavier gently tilted her face back up until she met his gaze once again. "You don't ever have to apologize for taking the time you need to become whole again."

"Whole again?" she whispered.

Xavier shrugged, nodding before he said, "A long time ago, just before mine and Aiden's eighth birthday, my father did something bad, Janie. Really bad. He sold out our pack for the chance to become alpha. He was the reason that so many people died, including my mother." Xavier pulled her closer, burying his face in her neck as he went on, "Afterwards, it felt as if I was torn into all of these separate, small pieces. I have worked hard to put all of those pieces back together again, and there are times where I still wonder if it will ever happen. I still don't understand how Chase could trust me and Aiden after my father got his parents killed. How everyone else in the pack can stand to look at us. How my Aunt Sadie, my mother's sister, could love us the way that she did when her husband was taken from her."

"Xavier, you were just a child. It wasn't your fault."

"I know," Xavier whispered, "but I can't help feeling the way that I do."

Janie stroked a hand down his hair, turning to kiss him gently on the cheek.

"I thought maybe that was what it felt like for you after everything you went through," Xavier continued, "and now you are working on putting the pieces back together."

"I never thought of it that way," Janie said softly, "but you are right. That's exactly how it feels."

"That's why I think it's important to take this slow," Xavier admitted, looking down into her eyes. "Your wolf accepts me, and a part of you does too. But I'm greedy sweetheart. I want all of you."

"I want that too," Janie whispered, leaning her forehead against his. "I want it all, Xavier." And she knew she had her work cut out for her if she was going to get it all, because Xavier was right. Until she opened up about what had happened to her when she was held by the General, until she was able to talk about the past, she would never be able to fully heal and give her mate the future that he deserved.

8

Xavier held Janie close while she slept, ignoring the dull ache in his lower back. He would suffer in silence, endure any pain he had to, as long as he had his woman in his arms. She was his miracle, his everything.

The door opened and Chase entered, Aiden right behind him. Xavier acknowledged his alpha's presence before turning to Aiden, "Where's Laynie?"

"Flame took her back to the apartment for now."

When Xavier would have protested, Chase cut in, "We have looked everywhere on White River Wolves land, Xavier. If Brent and his men were here, they aren't now."

Xavier relaxed some, shifting slightly to relieve some of the pressure on his back. "He won't stay gone long."

"Of that, I have no doubt," Chase agreed, "but we will be waiting for him next time."

"What's the plan?"

Chase rested his hands lightly on his hips and grinned. "The plan is for you to take the next few weeks off and get to know your mate, son." When Xavier stiffened, Chase held up a hand, "I apologize. I know you don't like it when I call you that."

Xavier felt Janie stir, and looked down to see her eyes on him. Slipping his fingers through her hair, he bent down to place a gentle kiss on her lips. "More pieces to put back together?" she questioned softly.

Xavier's gaze traveled over her delicate facial features, her eyes soft with understanding, and he nodded slowly. She was right. If she was going to do what she could on her end, then he needed to be willing to do the same. Raising his head, he met his alpha's gaze as he said, "After what the man I knew as my father did to this pack, his family, I have had a hard time understanding why anyone would want to use that term when it comes to myself or my brother."

"Don't you think you have carried that guilt around long enough, Xavier?" Chase asked quietly. "Your father's actions were not your own."

"I know."

"You need to learn to forgive him, Xavier."

"Forgive a monster?" Xavier growled. "My mother is dead because of him! Your parents are gone, and it is all his fault!"

Chase crossed the room and settled a hand firmly on his shoulder. "You can't live your life full of hate, son. Your father made a mistake. One that he paid deeply for in the end."

"What do you mean?" Xavier sighed as he felt Chase push some of his power his way, calming him and easing the pent-up pain he had held inside for years. When normally he would have rejected the warmth, this time he lowered his head and accepted it, letting it sink deep into his soul.

"Alpha?" Aiden said, taking a step in their direction, "what happened? How did our father pay for his sins, besides with his life?"

"Titen wanted power, so much so, that he allowed his desire for it to consume him. What he did not realize was everything it would end up costing him." Chase cursed quietly, looking from Aiden to Xavier. "I never wanted you to know what really happened. I tried to keep it from you, because I didn't want you to be hurt more than you already were."

"What?" Xavier demanded. What could be worse than everything they already knew?

"When we were attacked, your father knew it was coming, so he hid you boys in the crawl space above your bedroom. He told your mother to stay in the house, no matter what happened. He loved you all, and in his way, was trying to protect you." Chase paused, rubbing a hand over his face. "Your mother was nine months pregnant at the time. A baby girl. Lila hid the best she could, but the other pack turned on your father. They came to the house looking for all of you. When we got there, your mother was dead and your sister was gone."

"What?" Xavier gasped.

"Your father went crazy when he found out what happened," Chase went on. "He turned rogue, and became very dangerous. We had to track him down and kill him. We had no choice. He was murdering innocent people in his grief."

"We have a sister," Aiden whispered in shock.

Chase nodded. "Yes."

"Why didn't you tell us?" Xavier asked, his heart clenching at the thought of a young woman out there somewhere, his sister, scared and alone.

"Because no matter how hard I have tried, I can't find her," Chase admitted. "As the years went by without a trace, I thought it might be better to just keep quiet. You have both been through enough pain."

Xavier was aware of Janie gently stroking his chest, trying to soothe him, but all he could think of was his sister. "What if she needs us?" He could barely get the words out. He may not have known about her before, but she was still his little sister. His family. He couldn't just leave her out there on her own somewhere.

"Maybe she has a family," Janie suggested softly. "Maybe someone took her in that loves her."

"I hope so," Xavier muttered.

"What about RARE?" Aiden asked suddenly. "Isn't that what they do? Track down people that no one else can? Maybe they have contacts you don't? Maybe they can find our sister?"

Chase froze, his eyebrows drawing together into a deep frown, "Why the hell didn't I think of that?" he growled in frustration. "Angel is off the grid right now. She and her team are out looking for Jeremiah, but I will talk to her as soon as she gets back."

Xavier let out a breath he hadn't realized he was holding. "Thank you, Alpha."

Chase squeezed his shoulder once before letting go. "I just wish there was more I could do. I have exhausted any leads that I had, but maybe RARE will get further than I could."

"Who else knows about this?" Xavier asked, suspicion

beginning to fill him. How many people had lied to them over the years? It wasn't that he didn't understand why Chase made the decisions that he did, but did the entire pack know?

"Not many," Chase said. "Your aunt did, Doc Josie, a couple of the older wolves, and Sable."

"Sable knows and didn't tell me?" Aiden said, the hurt obvious in his voice. Besides Xavier, Sable was Aiden's best friend. They did everything together. At one time Xavier had wondered if Sable was Aiden's mate, but once he met Janie, he knew she couldn't be. There was no way they could be around each other as much as they were if they were mates, and not complete the bond. He had no idea how he had lasted a full year. Even now, he was fighting the urge to go back on his words of just an hour ago and claim her.

"She was under orders not to, Aiden," Chase told him, as he walked over to the door. "She didn't have a choice. She wanted to tell you, but I wouldn't allow it."

"Why does she know?" Xavier asked, his eyes on his brother.

"Sable walked into my office one day when I had a file open on my desk with your family's information in it. She saw enough that I had to tell her. Since then, she has been doing everything she can to help me find your sister. She wants to do it for you, but also for your sister. She says no one deserves to be lost."

"She's right," Janie whispered, bringing her hand up to clasp his tightly. "We need to find your sister."

AFTER LEAVING Xavier's hospital room, Chase slowly made his way back to his office, lost in thought. Xavier and Aiden's parents had been good friends with his own. They'd spent a lot of time together when Chase and Jenna were growing up. He even remembered calling them aunt and uncle. Killing Titen was one of the hardest things he'd ever had to do, but he did it for his pack.

Entering his office, Chase kicked the door shut behind him and walked over to look out the window. It was his fault that the twins had been left without a parent, but he would do it again if he had to. He was Alpha, which meant he had to make decisions sometimes that even he didn't like. For the better of his pack.

Sighing, Chase reached into his pocket and retrieved his cell phone. Xavier and Aiden had lost so much, and he refused to let Xavier lose anything else. He would do everything in his power to make sure Janie was safe, even if that meant calling in a favor to the one person who already carried the weight of the world on his shoulders.

The phone rang twice before a deep voice answered, "Jinx."

Chase's grip tightened on the phone as he closed his eyes and gritted his teeth. Jinx was his mate's son, now his son, and the only one who could help him. Chase was sure he knew Brent and would be able to track the bastard down. "I need a favor."

There was a slight pause before Jinx responded. "Name it."

9

Janie sat in front of Doc Josie's desk, tapping her fingers nervously on the arm of the chair as she waited for the doctor to arrive. It had been two weeks since Xavier was shot. Fourteen days spent with her mate, getting to know him, while trying to ignore the underlying sexual tension between them. She wanted him, needed him, but there was one thing holding them both back from sealing their bond. She was ready to tackle that issue now. She refused to allow her fear of the past to keep her from reaching for the future she dreamed about.

"Janie?" She heard the surprise in Josie's voice as she entered the room. Crossing quickly over to her desk, the doctor sat down in the chair behind it, her eyes narrowing on Janie. "Did we have an appointment? I'm so sorry if I'm late."

"No," Janie interjected quietly, "we didn't. But I was hoping you might have some free time for me today?"

A gentle smile curved Doc Josie's lips, as she replied, "Of course. I always have time for you, Janie."

Janie crossed her legs, clasping her hands tightly together. She wasn't sure how to start. How did you tell someone your deepest, darkest secrets? How did you admit the disgust and shame that swamped you every time you thought about not only how your daughter was conceived, but who her father was? Her eyes narrowed when another thought hit her. Was the doctor the one she should be telling these things to? She had chosen Josie because she trusted her...but there was someone else who really needed to hear what she was about to say. Raising her eyes to meet Josie's gaze, she whispered, "I wanted to talk to you, but..."

Josie waited for Janie to continue, but when she didn't, the doctor suggested, "How about we start with something easy? Let's talk about Alayna. How is she doing?"

Relief filled Janie at the small reprieve she was given, and she began to calm down slightly. "Laynie," she said softly.

"Laynie?"

Janie felt her face flush with pleasure as she thought about how close Xavier and her daughter had become over the past few days. "It's what Xavier calls her. He is wonderful with Alayna. He just claimed her as his own, right away."

"That's what shifters do," Josie told her softly. "You are his mate, which means Alayna is his daughter now, too."

"Not all shifters," Janie said quietly.

"What do you mean?"

"Let's just say, in my old pack things were run differently. They would not have accepted my daughter. They would have never allowed me to bring her back there to be raised." Janie clenched her teeth, fighting back tears that had suddenly filled her eyes. "I guess I don't have to worry about that, though."

"No, Janie, you don't," Doc Josie agreed. They had spoken in the past about Janie's family and old alpha, so Josie already knew the history behind her remark. Instead of dwelling on those painful memories, Josie leaned forward, resting her arms on the desk as she changed the subject. "Tell me, what else have you been up to these past few days?"

Janie picked at the hem of her shirt as she responded, "I've been taking lessons."

"Lessons?"

"Shooting and sparring lessons," Janie told her. "Flame's been teaching me."

Josie's eyebrows rose in surprise. "Really?

"I'm not like Flame, though," Janie said. "I'm not looking for revenge, Josie. I just want to live my life. But, to do that, I need to learn how to protect myself and my child. I know Xavier will when he's around, but when he's not," Janie shrugged, "it's up to me."

"You and the pack," Josie replied. "We will all protect both you and Alayna."

"I know," Janie whispered, her heart full of love for the people who had taken her in, giving her a home when she had none. "I know that now." The White River Wolves had all come together, offering their protection with the threat of Brent still there. They took turns standing outside her apartment at night, two right outside her door, and several surrounding the building. Xavier was always right below her bedroom window. She had tried to tell him that he needed to go home and get some rest, but he refused to leave her. When she asked him if he would like to stay in the apartment with her, he told her not yet. He would be tempted to do things that he knew they were not ready for right now. Which brought her thoughts back to the reason she was really there. Taking a deep breath, she swallowed hard and then began, "The General's men found me when I was living in a small town in California."

She saw Doc Josie's eyes widened in surprise at the direction the conversation had taken.

"I was working at a small diner as a waitress," Janie continued, her voice low. "I was alone, kicked out of my pack. I had no one."

Janie began to tremble, and she took several deep breaths to try and calm herself. Josie stood, coming around the desk to sit in the chair beside her. The doctor's hands covered hers as she asked quietly, "Would you like me to get Jade?"

"No," Janie whispered. "Please, I trust you." It wasn't that she didn't trust Jade. But Doc Josie had been there from the day she first arrived at the compound. And right now, she was the only one Janie wanted to share her story with.

"Are you sure?"

Janie began to tremble harder, her whole body shaking as the memories slammed into her, one after another. No, she didn't want Jade there, but there was someone that she needed. Raising her eyes to meet the doctor's, Janie whispered, "Xavier. Please, call Xavier."

Josie nodded, quickly taking out her cell phone and placing the call. Then she sat with Janie in silence until

Xavier appeared in the doorway just a few minutes later. He was at her side instantly, kneeling to take her hand in his. "Sweetheart, what's wrong?"

Janie looked into his deep brown eyes, eyes so full of love, even if he hadn't said the words to her just yet. He was everything that she had always dreamed of in a mate, and so much more. Reaching out, she slowly brushed a lock of his hair back from his forehead as she whispered, "It was so dark that night when they came to the diner where I was working. I knew right away that something was wrong with them." She felt Xavier stiffen, his hand tightening on hers, but she could not stop the words from falling out of her mouth now. "They followed me home. I couldn't get away. I tried. I never stopped trying. The General paired me with Brent. He hurt me, Xavier. He took from me everything that should have been yours. Over and over and over again. It got to be that I would pray that the General would send him away on an assignment. I'm such a horrible person. I didn't even care where he was going or who he might hurt. I just wanted him gone."

"You are not a horrible person, my sweet mate," Xavier rasped, his hand coming up to gently stroke her cheek.

"I thought it would finally stop when I got pregnant," Janie went on, pushing the words out. "I thought it would be over because I was finally going to have a baby, which was what they wanted, but I was wrong. It only got worse. He moved me to that place in Mexico. There, it wasn't just Brent that took me. I was pregnant, but none of them cared. They just hurt me over and over again."

Xavier swore darkly, moving closer to pull her into his arms. Janie laid her head on his shoulder and cried as he gently stroked her back, placing soft kisses on the top of her head. "Nobody will ever hurt you again," he promised. "I will fucking kill anybody who lays a hand on you. I promise you that, baby."

A cry tore from Janie's throat, deep heart-wrenching sobs coming from deep within her chest. "It seemed like the pain never went away, Xavier. Not until they brought me here." She cried for several minutes, until she had no more tears left. Then she leaned back and looked at him. Cradling his face in the palms of her hands, she whispered, "I felt lost and alone for so long, Xavier. Terrified of my own shadow. And then I had Alayna, and I knew I had to become the person that I used to be. I had to take care of her, protect her. I couldn't let myself be the weak, pitiful version of who I was after the General took me." She stared deeply into his eyes as a tremulous smile crossed her lips. "Each day I fought to become stronger for Alayna, but I was still so alone. Even surrounded by everyone here at the compound. And then, one day, I ran into you."

Xavier leaned forward and gently kissed the tears from her cheeks. "I remember that day clearly," he said softly. "Your hair was down, with big curls I wanted to wrap around my fingers. Your eyes were so sad, and I wanted to chase away all of your demons. You were so beautiful, and I wanted nothing more than to talk to you, but you turned and ran."

Janie blushed, ducking her head shyly. "I knew who you were, but I had nothing to offer you then, Xavier. I watched you, though. I even asked Flame about you. And I knew that you were there for me, every night when you were home, underneath my window. I hated it when you were gone. I couldn't sleep."

"I'm so sorry," Xavier said.

"It's not your fault. It's your job. I just…I missed you. Each day after that, the loneliness began to fade away, and my heart began to fill." Janie was aware that Doc Josie rose and left the room then, shutting the door quietly behind her. But she never took her gaze from the man who still knelt in front of her. "You hold my heart in your hands, Xavier Andrews. You saved me when I didn't think I could ever be saved. You are my light, my love, my salvation. My heart belongs to you."

Xavier closed the distance between them, gently covering her lips with his. She felt a shudder run through his body as he held her close. Finally, he pulled back, their eyes meeting as he told her, "You have owned my heart since the first day I saw you, Janie. I love you so much, baby."

Janie slid her arms around Xavier's neck, tugging him close, sighing softly. "I love you, too."

10

Jinx jumped into the air, grasping one of the lower tree branches and swinging himself up onto it. Quickly, he climbed higher, scaling one branch after another, until he was just over halfway up the tree. When he found the one he wanted, he sat, letting his legs dangle over the side. Raising an eyebrow, he glanced at the makeshift campsite below. Four sleeping bags were positioned around a fire pit, empty beer cans and trash littering the area. There were a couple of duffle bags near two coolers, open with clothes falling out. Fucking pigs.

Taking out his phone, Jinx sent a quick text to his person on the inside, following up on the General's medical status. After being nearly mauled to death just weeks before by Chase, the General was slowly beginning to recover. As much as Jinx hated the man, it made his life easier to keep him alive right now. He was trying to find out who the head prick in charge was, and with the General injured, it was proving to be even more difficult than when he was running around throwing out asshole orders left and right. Jinx waited impatiently until the response came back. *The same.* Good, at least he wasn't dead just yet. He would be one day though, after his neck met Jinx's sword.

Quickly shoving the phone back into his pocket at the sound of voices heading his way, Jinx stared at the forest floor below. It hadn't taken him long to find Brent and his band of dumbasses. They were hiding out in the mountains not far from the White River Wolves compound. It was further than Chase's enforcers would have looked, which was why their trackers weren't able to scent them, but Jinx had his own way of tracking his prey. And he always found what he was hunting.

"How much longer do we have to stay up here, Brent?" one of the men grumbled, following Brent into the small clearing.

"Until I tell you we don't," Brent snapped, walking under the tree Jinx was in.

"Fuck, I say we go into town tonight," another guy said, stalking over to where one of the sleeping bags lay out on the ground. One hand clutching a rifle tightly, he turned around to look at the rest of them as he crudely grabbed his dick. "It's been a long time since I've had a good steak and a sweet piece of ass."

"And it is going to be even longer," Brent snarled. "Nobody is leaving this fucking mountain until I get what I came for."

Jinx pushed off the branch and landed lightly on his feet, just inches from one of the men. "You have part of that right," he commented dryly, drawing his sword from its scabbard at his back. "None of you are leaving this mountain."

11

Xavier swore softly when there was a loud knock on his apartment door. He had just finished packing a bag, and was getting ready to head over to Janie's place to stay with her. She'd finally let him in, allowing him to see a part of her that she had never shared before, and he refused to leave her alone tonight after the way she bared her soul. Whoever was on the other side of that door wasn't staying long.

"I got it," Aiden said, as he walked past Xavier's bedroom in just a pair of loose shorts. His brother was going to take his place at the bottom of Janie's window. Xavier didn't fully trust anyone except Aiden to protect them while they slept.

Grabbing his duffle bag, Xavier took one last look around his room. If things went the way he wanted them to, he would only be back to collect the rest of his things. He didn't plan on waiting much longer to claim his mate, and once he did, there was no way he was going to be apart from her again.

Xavier quickly scanned the living room when he walked in, unable to stop the smile that appeared when he saw Janie sitting on the couch. She'd come to the apartment with him to get his things, but insisted on waiting in the front room, not wanting to invade Aiden's space. "You ready, sweetheart?" he asked quietly, closing the distance between them and leaning down to place a soft kiss on her lips. Her quiet response was drowned out by his alpha's voice.

"I'm glad you are here, Janie. I need to speak to both you and Xavier."

Janie turned to look at Chase, and Xavier stiffened when he saw her eyes widen in surprise as she reached out to grab his hand. Dropping his bag, he sat down beside her and slipped his arm around her, drawing her close before looking over at his alpha. Standing next to Chase was Angel's son, Jinx. A low growl built in his throat when he felt Janie begin to tremble in his arms.

"Stand down, Xavier," Chase growled, his clear blue eyes darkening in anger. "You will treat my son with respect."

"He's scaring my mate," Xavier snarled, baring his teeth.

"No," Janie whispered, grasping his arm tightly, "Jinx doesn't scare me."

Xavier looked down in confusion, anger still flowing through him. "You're shaking, Janie. I can smell your fear."

"I'm not afraid of him," Janie insisted, raising a hand to rest it on his chest. "It's just hard to separate him from the General sometimes," she admitted, looking over at Jinx. "I'm sorry. We never met when I was being held captive, but I heard about you. Some of the women would whisper about the man who helped them without the General knowing. Going so far as to rescue a few of the lucky ones." Lowering her eyes, she whispered, "Sometimes I wished it was me that you helped, but I knew you couldn't save all of us."

"I would if I could," Jinx said, slowly walking over to kneel in front of her. "I can't let the General find out what I do. If too many women go missing, he will start asking questions."

Janie nodded, "I know."

"I did help you though, Janie," Jinx told her, "and with your mate's permission, I would like to show you."

Xavier's eyes narrowed on the man, his arm tightening around his mate. "What do you mean?"

"Janie will only believe me if she sees it for herself," Jinx told him calmly. "I can show her, if you would allow it. I promise, no harm will come to her."

Xavier looked down at Janie, a silent question in his eyes. He didn't have all of the facts, but he knew that some of the new members of his pack had special abilities, psychic gifts they used to help others. Could Jinx have some of the same gifts?

Janie's eyes met his and she nodded. Taking a deep breath, Xavier muttered, "Do it."

JANIE'S GAZE never left Jinx as he slowly lifted his hands and cupped her face in his palms. "Close your eyes, sweet wolf," he said softly. "I am going to show you that you are finally free to spend the rest of your life without fear."

"Wolf?"

Jinx smiled, "She's in there just waiting to come out," he said. "You know it, too. She will show herself to everyone soon." Nodding toward Xavier, he said, "She has a very good reason now."

Janie's lips trembled as she returned Jinx's smile. Then she gasped as images started to flood her mind. Closing her eyes, she shuddered, moaning softly when she saw Jinx wielding a sword as it sliced through a man's neck. Then a knife flew from Jinx's hand, and was embedded into another man's chest. "You bastard! The General will hear about this!"

"Oh, God," Janie whimpered, trying to pull free of the vision. It was Brent. He felt so close.

Hush, little one. Jinx's voice broke through her terror. *He will never hurt you again. Watch.*

Janie forced herself to become calm, small whimpers escaping her throat as she watched the scene play out before her.

"Who's going to tell him?" Jinx asked, raising an eyebrow as a slow grin crossed his lips. "You?" Shaking his head, Jinx raised his sword and pointed it at Brent. "You won't be around to tell him anything, Brent. You will never threaten another person, never hurt another woman. Janie will be free of you."

"Why the fuck do you care about that little bitch?" Brent said, swiftly pulling a gun from the back of his jeans. "Who is she to you?"

Jinx seemed to pause for a moment, before he replied, "She's of the same pack, which makes her family. No one will ever touch her again."

A shot rang out, but it was too late. The bullet went wide as Jinx swung his sword.

Janie slowly came back to herself, opening eyes that

were wet with tears. She was aware of Xavier's arm around her, but she only had eyes for Jinx. "So many times I prayed you would save me...and you did."

Jinx let his hands drop from her cheeks, his dark brown eyes guarded as he sat back on his heels. He gave her a short nod.

"Will the General be coming for me?" she asked cautiously, moving to the edge of the couch, closer to him.

"No," Jinx promised, and she could tell that it was the truth. "The General isn't going after anyone right now. And when he is ready to, you won't be on his list to hunt down."

Janie didn't bother trying to hide the tears streaming down her face as she leaned forward and wrapped her arms around the man in front of her, burying her face in his neck as she clung to him. "You told him no one would ever hurt me again," she whispered, "and you meant it. I heard it in your voice. You said we are of the same pack. Family."

She felt Jinx run a hand gently down her hair before pulling back. "The White River Wolves are the closest thing I have to a pack," he admitted. "And my dad always told me that everyone in a pack watches over each other."

"Your dad was right," Chase said, as he came to stand near them. "And you *are* a part of this pack, Jinx."

Jinx stood, but not before Janie saw what she swore was a sheen of tears in his eyes. "I have to go," he told them. "I have a mission I need to fulfill before I go back."

"Thank you," Janie said, rising from the couch. "You don't know what you have done for me. For my daughter."

Jinx gave her one last small smile before turning to

leave. Aiden moved to block his way. Standing tall and proud, he said, "My brother's mate has lived here for over a year, terrified that the General and his men were going to come for her. Today, you did something none of us have been able to do. You wiped that terror from her eyes. My family is indebted to you, my friend. If you ever need anything, and I mean anything, you call me. I will be there."

"That goes for me, too," Xavier said gruffly from beside her.

Jinx looked down at the hand Aiden held out to him, then back at Xavier. Swallowing hard, he reached out and accepted the handshake. "I will accept your friendship, but there is no debt to repay."

"You call," Aiden said again, "and we will be there, Jinx. As friends and as pack."

Janie clasped Xavier's hand tightly in hers as she watched Jinx nod, then leave without a backward glance. He had just saved her life, and the life of her child. She did not care what he said, she owed him a debt that she could never hope to repay.

12

After leaving Xavier's apartment the hour before, Xavier and Janie had arrived at hers to find Flame's bags packed and sitting by the front door. Against Janie's objections, Flame told them she was moving out to give them more room. She had been offered one of the empty places just two doors down, but Flame said she had refused, deciding to stay out at Angel's house instead. It stood empty since Angel moved in with Chase, and Flame insisted she wanted the privacy. She would be back the following evening for the rest of her things, but for now, Xavier and Janie were alone. She just needed to get her daughter to bed, and then they would have a chance to talk...or something.

Janie took a deep breath as she looked around the dimly lit room. Alayna snored softly in her crib, oblivious to the tension running through her mother. It was her daughter's first night in her new bedroom, and Janie was finding it so hard to leave her alone, even though she knew the threat to their lives had been removed.

"Everything okay?" Xavier asked quietly from behind her. Janie turned to look at him, unsure how to respond. His eyes narrowed, and he took a step toward her. "Sweetheart, nothing has to happen tonight. I can sleep in the living room if you would like? I will even change into my wolf if it would make you feel more comfortable."

"It's not that," Janie interrupted.

"Then what is it?" he asked, reaching out to slip a piece of her long hair behind her ear. "You can tell me anything, Janie."

"I know," she whispered, looking back at Alayna. The moon shone through the blinds, resting on her daughter's small features. "It's just that I have never been without her at night," she finally said. "What if something happens?"

"Baby," Xavier said, sliding his arms around her waist and pulling her close, "nothing is going to happen. She is right next to our room. We will hear her if she needs us."

"I know," Janie sighed, looking up at him through lowered lids. "I just worry."

"Do you want to bring her back in with us?" he offered, kissing her softly on the forehead. "We could put the crib back where it was until you are ready for her to be in here."

Janie's eyes widened in surprise, shocked that he would be willing to do that for her. She could feel the evidence of his arousal pressing insistently against her belly, but instead of trying to coerce her with sex, he was doing everything he could to make her happy. Just like he always did. He never worried about himself, it was always about her and Alayna.

With one last glance at her daughter, who was snuggled deep in her covers sleeping peacefully, Janie slipped out of Xavier's arms and captured one of his hands in hers. After making sure the lights were off in the rest of the apartment, she led him back to her bedroom, their bedroom now, shutting the door behind them.

Letting go of him, Janie walked over to stand in front of the bed. "Janie?" he whispered raggedly, as she grasped the bottom of her shirt and slowly slid it up and over her head. His gaze locked on her light pink bra, and she heard a low growl escape his throat. "Janie," he rasped, "don't take off anything else unless you are ready for what's going to happen next. I don't have the energy or control to hold back much longer."

"So don't," she whispered, slipping her fingers into the waistband of her leggings and sliding them down over her hips. Her lacy pink underwear hugged her body, accenting her slender hips, with a golden heart charm hanging down in the front, resting against the curve of her mound. After kicking the leggings off, Janie raised her eyes to look at his, biting her bottom lip nervously.

"Fuck, Janie, you know what that does to me," Xavier ground out roughly as he quickly crossed the room to her. His lips were on hers, her body flush against his, before she knew what was happening. He ground his hips into hers, his hard length pushing into her, and a small squeak left her lips as she grasped his shirt tightly and pressed closer to him.

"If you want me to stop, you have to tell me now, baby," Xavier snarled, tilting his head back from her, sucking in deep breaths of air.

"If I wanted you to stop, I would never have started this in the first place," Janie growled, satisfaction filling her as she watched her nails begin to grow and felt her fangs fill her mouth. She was ready to claim her mate, and nothing was going to stop her. One way or another, he would be hers by the next morning. Very carefully, she swiped her claws down his shirt, effectively removing it from his body. "You are mine," she murmured, running her hands up and over his hard chest. "Mine!"

"Fuck, yes," Xavier rasped, settling his hands on her hips and pulling her up against him again. "I'm yours."

Janie reached down and undid the button on his jeans, then slid the zipper down. Shoving them down his legs, along with his boxers, she soon had him standing fully naked in front of her. His hard cock was between them, and she reached down to wrap her fingers around it. He gasped, and she slowly slid her fingers up and down his length. Her body shook with need, a feeling she had never felt before, but there was also a small tinge of fear that she couldn't seem to block out. Even though she'd had sex in the past, none of it had been consensual, and all of it had been painful. She wanted to claim Xavier, and she was going to, but a part of her was scared that it would hurt, just like before.

Xavier must have scented her fear, because suddenly his hand closed over hers and he pulled it away from him. "Stop, sweetheart," he said, bringing her hand up and kissing it gently. "It's okay. You don't have to."

Tears filled her eyes as she whispered, "I want to, Xavier. Every part of me wants to. I'm just scared."

"We will wait," Xavier muttered, rubbing his cheek against her hand. "We don't have to do this now. All that matters is that you are here with me. Everything else can wait."

"I don't want to wait, Xavier," Janie insisted, sliding her

hand into his thick hair. "I want you. I need to know what it feels like to share something like this with someone you love. It's just that…" she paused, meeting his gaze before going on, "it always hurt before. All I know is pain. I don't want to feel pain. I want pleasure." Tightening her hand in his hair, she pulled his head down to hers. Brushing her lips lightly over his, she whispered, "Show me what love feels like, Xavier."

———————

XAVIER GROANED when his lips met Janie's. A part of him wanted to yell and scream, then go and kill every single person who had been a part of what happened to his woman. But he knew that wasn't what Janie needed right now.

Pushing down all of his anger, he vowed to show her the patience and love she deserved. Running his fingers softly down her arms, he lightly traced her lips with his tongue. He fought for control as she panted against his mouth. She wanted him, he could feel it, taste it. Inhaling deeply, he let the smell of her desire run through him, the scent of her fear reminding him that she needed gentleness above all else right now.

Bending, Xavier slid an arm under Janie's legs and slowly lifted her into his arms, swallowing her gasp of surprise. Gently he set her down in the middle of the bed, and then followed her onto it. Letting his gaze wander down her body and then back up, he stifled a groan at the way her bra cupped her breasts firmly, and the way her panties barely hid what was beneath them. Her skin was a milky white color, so soft to the touch, and he wanted to trace every inch of it with his tongue.

"Xavier," Janie panted, "please." Her beautiful eyes were wide with desire, her lips slightly parted as she stared at him in confused expectation. She had no idea what she was asking for, and that pissed him off. She was his, dammit, and the things she had gone through were so horrible, his gut twisted in horror and anger every time he thought of it. His mate, his everything, forced to do things no one should ever be forced to do. He hoped he could give her everything she needed.

Leaning down, he kissed her gently, nibbling lightly on her bottom lip. Sliding his hand over the silky skin on her stomach, he slowly moved it up to cup her breast. Deepening the kiss, he swallowed her moan of pleasure as he skimmed his thumb over her nipple.

"Xavier!" His name was a plea against his lips as she pushed into his hand. Her body trembled against him, her hands gripping his shoulders as she tried to pull him closer.

Slowly, he moved his hand up and slid her bra straps down. First one, and then the other. Reaching behind her, he undid the hooks at her back, before removing the bra and tossing it to the floor. Lowering his head, Xavier licked one of her nipples before sucking it into his mouth. Janie cried out, arching off the bed. "That's it, sweetheart," he rasped, pulling back to blow lightly on her nipple before moving over to the other one to give it the same attention.

His gums ached, the need to sink his teeth deep into her soft skin and claim her was beating at him, but he pushed it down. This was for her. He could smell her arousal, knew she wanted him, but that slight bit of fear was still there, floating around them.

"You are so beautiful, Janie," he whispered, leaving her breasts to lightly lick and kiss his way down her stomach. Slipping his fingers into the sides of her underwear, he slowly slid them down her thighs as he sucked gently on the skin right above her belly button.

"Xavier," she moaned, moving her head from side to side on the pillow, "I don't know what to do."

"You don't have to do anything, baby," he muttered, swirling his tongue down low on her belly, "just let go and enjoy everything. I've got you."

"Xavier!" she screamed, as he ducked his head and flicked her clit with the tip of his tongue. Gripping her hips gently in his hands, he licked her, a low growl ripping from him when her taste exploded on his tongue. His fangs punched through his gums and he fought for control, not wanting to scare her.

"Hold still for a second, baby," he urged, resting his head on Janie's belly.

"I can't!" she protested, lifting her hips up as she slid her fingers into his hair. Gripping the strands tightly, she guided his mouth back to her. "Please…"

He couldn't resist. Finding her clit, he began to lick and suck, the sounds she was making driving him out of his mind. He ground his hard cock into the mattress, trying to find some relief as he pushed Janie over the edge into an orgasm. Her fingers pulled his hair as her soft cries filled the room.

Raising his head, Xavier looked up into her wide eyes,

dark with desire. He couldn't wait any longer. Slowly, he crawled up her body, covering it with his. Placing his arms on either side of her head, he leaned in and kissed her. He rested his forehead against hers, looking deep into her eyes. "I love you, Janie," he rasped, as he found her entrance with his aching cock, and slowly began to push inside. "You are my world, my everything."

He saw tears fill her eyes, and tried to pull back, but she shook her head. "No," she whispered, "don't stop."

"I don't want to hurt you."

Janie smiled, running her hands up and down his back. "You aren't hurting me, Xavier," she whispered, as one tear slipped free. "You are loving me."

Xavier swallowed hard, closing his eyes for a moment, then opening them to lock with hers again. "Always." Gritting his teeth, he cupped her head in the palms of his hands and then began to move slowly.

He watched her closely, but all he saw was pleasure. The fear was gone. Her eyes darkened even more, and she began to meet him thrust for thrust. Suddenly, a low growl slipped from Janie, and he felt sharp claws dig into his ass as she bared her teeth, her eyes beginning to glow a dark topaz. "Mine!" she growled, right before she moved her head and sank her fangs into his shoulder.

"Fuck! Janie!" He couldn't have held back after that if he tried. But he didn't try. He lowered his head and buried his own fangs into her silky skin, groaning as he came deep inside her. He felt the moment their souls were melded together as one, as they were meant to be. The bond clicked into place, and a peace like no other filled him.

Pulling his teeth from her shoulder, Xavier licked at his mating mark. "Mine," he muttered, kissing it gently before meeting her gaze.

"Always," Janie replied, her eyes lit with love, a soft smile on her lips.

13

R eaching into the crib, Janie tucked the small blanket around her daughter, a small smile crossing her lips. Xavier had gone to get some more things from his apartment, and Flame was getting ready to leave with what was left of hers. She would miss her friend, but she was excited to begin the rest of her life with Xavier.

Shivering at the sudden chill in the air, Janie crossed to the other side of the room and gently lowered the window, wondering how it had gotten so cold so quickly. It took her a moment to realize that it couldn't be coming from Alayna's window. It had only been open a small crack.

With one last look at her daughter, Janie left the room and wandered slowly down the hall. She paused when she reached the living room, her brow furrowing as she glanced around the small apartment, taking in the open sliding glass doors to the balcony. "Flame? Is that you?"

When there was no response, Janie glanced back

toward her daughter's room, debating on calling Xavier, but then she noticed something in the air that she had missed when she first came into the room. Blood. Flame's blood.

Quickly making her way across the living room, Janie gasped when she saw her friend lying unconscious on the kitchen floor, blood streaming from her temple and dripping on the white tile. A gun lay beside her, as if it had slipped out of her grasp when she fell. "Flame!" she gasped in shock, running to crouch beside her. Feeling desperately for a pulse, Janie shuddered in relief when she found a strong one.

She was so worried about Flame, that she almost missed the familiar smell that suddenly teased her nostrils. One she hadn't scented in a very long time. Inhaling deeply, just to verify what she already knew, Janie rose, turning to face the man who now stood in front of her. "What are you doing here?" she demanded.

"I made a mistake, Janie. I'm here to take you home."

"A mistake? How did you find me?"

"Let's just say I have friends in high places," was the short response. "Time to go."

Janie shook her head slowly. "No. I won't go with you."

The man's eyes narrowed, and he grinned ruefully. "You sound like you think you have a choice. You should know better than that by now, girl." Pulling a gun from behind his back, he pointed it at Flame. "Now, let's go, unless you prefer I put a bullet in your friend here."

Janie swallowed hard, her gaze going from Flame, then down the hall to where her baby slept peacefully in her crib, and back to the man in front of her. His eyes narrowed as he watched her carefully, "Or maybe there is something else in this place that means more to you?"

Janie stiffened, realizing her mistake immediately. He obviously didn't know about Alayna, and she didn't want him to. She moved quickly to stand in front of Flame, hoping to distract him from the little girl who owned her heart. Gritting her teeth, she growled, "I will not let you hurt my friend." *Or my daughter*, she thought as her eyes strayed to the gun on the floor just a few feet from her.

He threw his head back and laughed. "Do you really think you will be fast enough, girl? I will shoot that bitch first, and then go after whatever waits down that hall. Smells like a child to me. Your child."

Anger filled Janie, pure raw fury. She was going to kill the bastard for threatening her daughter. The pain hit her hard, her body suddenly bending and reforming like it had never done before. Claws sprang from her nails, and fur began to sprout on the back of her hands, then down her arms.

"What the hell?" he yelled, his eyes wide with shock. "You can't fucking shift!"

"I guess I can now, asshole," Janie snarled around a mouthful of teeth. Dropping to her knees, she groaned as her bones began to change and transform into something she never thought possible. It didn't take long, and soon she was standing on all four legs, shaking out of what was left of her clothes, glaring at the man in front of her. She hated him. Had always hated him. And now he had just made the fatal mistake of threatening her daughter.

He threw his head back and laughed. "This just means I will get just as much money for you as I did your sister," he said, taking a step toward her. "She didn't come easily either, but she soon figured out that you can't fight your alpha. I will always win."

The door to the apartment opened, and that small distraction was all Janie needed. Leaping at Byron Reed, she wrapped her jaws around his neck and clamped down hard. She had seen his eyes widen in surprise, but he never got a chance to react. It was over within seconds, with her old alpha on the ground, his throat ripped out, and Janie standing over him. Her body shook as she stared at him, thinking about the hell she'd lived through for so long after he kicked her out of his pack.

"Holy shit. Your mate is badass, X."

The sound of Aiden's voice pulled her out of the rage she was in. Her gaze swinging toward the door, she cocked her head to the side. Xavier, Aiden, and Chase stood just inside the room, their arms full of boxes. His eyes never leaving hers, Xavier let his box drop to the floor. "It's okay, baby," he said quietly, crossing the floor to kneel beside her. Reaching out, he ran a hand gently over her head and down her back. "Your wolf is gorgeous, mate. I've never seen a wolf with fur that beautiful tawny color like yours before. It has small pieces of white throughout, and your eyes. They are breath-taking. A dark golden color." Janie's wolf preened at his words, and she rubbed her head against his chest. Xavier stroked his hand down her side, leaning in to kiss her muzzle gently. "I love your wolf, Janie, but I would like you to come back to me now, please."

Janie's eyes narrowed, and she looked over at Chase for help. She had no idea how she had shifted in the first place. How did she change back?

Chase smiled, setting the box in his hands on the

carpet before making his way toward her. "Let me help you, little wolf."

Janie felt his power pouring through her, filling her with contentment, along with a silent command, and then she was shifting. It took a while, and she shivered when she was finally fully back in human form, gratefully accepting the blanket Aiden wrapped around her.

"What the hell happened?" Janie's gaze flew to where Flame was pushing herself up into a sitting position on the kitchen floor, glaring around the room as she pressed a hand to the side of her head. "Someone fucking hit me with something. I'm going to kill him!"

"Good luck with that," Aiden laughed, motioning to where Byron lay in the middle of the living room floor. "Janie already beat you to it."

"Janie?" Flame asked, her eyes narrowing as she struggled to her feet with Chase's help.

"I guess my wolf didn't like him threatening you and Alayna," Janie said, burrowing into Xavier's side, exhaustion rolling through her after what she'd just been through.

"Who was he?" Chase broke in, after helping Flame over to the couch.

"My old alpha," Janie admitted, laying her head against Xavier's shoulder. "He said he made a mistake. That he came to take me home."

"A mistake?"

Janie's eyes widened in horror when she remembered his next words. "He said that since I could shift, he would be able to get just as much money for me as he did my sister." Grasping Xavier's shirt tightly in her hand, Janie looked at Chase. "He sold my sister, Alpha. Please, we have to find out where she is."

"We will, Janie," Chase promised, taking out his phone. "First, I am going to get someone in here to clean up this mess. Then, I'm going to need all the information you have on your sister, and I will contact your old pack to find out what they know. Don't worry, we will find her."

"We have to," Janie whispered, her gaze going to Xavier. "She was the only one who fought for me, Xavier. The only one who wanted me to stay. We have to find her."

"We will," he told her, cupping her face gently in his hand. "We will."

14

J anie sat on the bench in front of the hospital, Alayna in the stroller beside her. Xavier had left the week before with a team to find her sister, following up on some leads they'd gotten from her old pack. After they found out their alpha was dead, they'd all been more than happy to turn over any information they had to them. All except her parents. They refused to talk to anyone about either her or Silver. It had been two days since she'd spoken to her mate, and she was slowly going out of her mind with worry.

"It's going to be okay."

Janie turned to look at Jade, nodding with a small smile, even though she didn't really believe the other woman.

Jade sat down beside her, covering Janie's clasped hands with one of her own. "Trust me," she said softly, a gentle smile forming on her lips as she looked over toward the entrance to the compound.

Janie followed her gaze, stiffening when just moments

later a black SUV pulled up, waiting until the gate lifted before driving through. Janie stood, her hand now clutching Jade's tightly as she watched the SUV head their way, coming to a stop in front of the hospital. The driver's door opened, and Xavier stepped out, a wide grin on his face as he looked at her. Turning, he opened the door behind him, and someone slipped out. Janie gasped when she saw a head full of light blonde hair. When the door shut, her eyes connected with dark grey ones dancing with laughter. "Silver." She breathed her sister's name, taking a step toward her, her hand outstretched. She'd never thought she would see Silver again. Alpha Reed had been adamant about her not contacting anyone from the pack after she was kicked out. The punishment for defying his direct order was death.

Silver grinned, quickly closing the distance between them and wrapping Janie up in her arms. Janie clung to her, crying tears of pain and joy. Pain for all of the time missed with Silver, and joy that her sister was now there in her arms. "I've missed you so much," Silver whispered, holding her close. Leaning back, she smiled, "Thank you for sending your mate and his friends to find me."

Janie stiffened, her gaze sliding quickly over her sister. "Are you okay? Were you hurt?" She didn't look hurt. Silver was dressed in black leather, from head to toe. Janie's eyes widened when she saw the gun strapped to her side, and another on her thigh. She could see the hilt of a knife sticking out of her boot, and something shiny was hiding in pockets down the side of her pants. She didn't look like someone who needed rescuing. Far from it.

Silver laughed, shaking her head. "That stupid son of a

bitch Reed tried to sell me off to someone called the General. The same bastard who took you, from what Xavier told me. Unfortunately for him, the goons he sent didn't get very far. What you don't know, sis, is that I have been training to become an enforcer since you left. At least that is what our pack thought. Actually, I had really decided that I wasn't going to let anyone tell me what to do anymore. Asshole Reed was not going to control me. Once I thought I was ready and able to protect us both, I was coming for you. I didn't care if we had to live by ourselves. You are my sister, my best friend, and I love you."

Janie's eyes sparkled with tears as she murmured, "You always were the stronger one."

Silver threw back her head and laughed. "I don't know about that, sis," she scoffed. "I may have dreamed about taking out our alpha, but you are the one who actually accomplished it. Sounds to me like you are the strong one, Janie."

"Mama."

Alayna's soft voice interrupted them, and Silver's eyes softened as she turned to where she sat in her stroller, her arms stretched out toward Janie. "This must be Laynie. I've heard a lot about you, little one."

Janie moved to pick Alayna up, cuddling her close. "Meet Alayna Silver Andrews, your niece."

"Andrews?"

Xavier's rough whisper reached across the hospital gardens, and Janie smiled, watching him walk their way. "Alayna after my great grandmother, Silver after my sister, and every little girl should have their father's last name."

She saw the moisture in his eyes as he stopped in front of her, gathering them both in his arms. "Yes," he agreed gruffly, "yes, they should."

Janie snuggled into her mate's arms, glancing around at her sister and the other enforcers who stood near. This was her pack. These were her people. She finally had what she had always wanted. She was home. She was finally home.

Make sure and visit my website for information on all of my books, and to sign up for my Newsletter where you will receive all of the latest information on new releases, sales, and more!

Website: **http://www.dawnsullivanauthor.com/**

I would love to have you join my reader's group, Author Dawn Sullivan's RARE Rebels, so that we can hang out and chat, and where you will also get sneak peeks of cover reveals, read excerpts before anyone else, and more!

https://www.facebook.com/groups/AuthorDawnSullivan sRebelReaders/

Dawn Sullivan

ABOUT THE AUTHOR

Dawn Sullivan has a wonderful, supportive husband, and three beautiful children. She enjoys spending time with them, which normally involves some baseball, shooting hoops, taking walks, watching movies, and reading.

Her passion for reading began at a very young age and only grew over time. Whether she was bringing home a book from the library, or sneaking one of her mother's romance novels to read by the light in the hallway when she was supposed to be sleeping, Dawn always had a book. She reads several different genres and subgenres, but Paranormal Romance and Romantic Suspense are her favorites.

Dawn has always made up stories of her own, and finally decided to start sharing them with others. She hopes everyone enjoys reading them as much as she enjoys writing them.

facebook.com/dawnsullivanauthor

twitter.com/dawn_author

instagram.com/dawn_sullivan_author

OTHER BOOKS BY DAWN SULLIVAN

RARE Series

Book 1 Nico's Heart

Book 2 Phoenix's Fate

Book 3 Trace's Temptation

Book 4 Saving Storm

Book 5 Angel's Destiny

White River Wolves Series

Book 1 Josie's Miracle

Book 2 Slade's Desire

Book 3 Janie's Salvation

Serenity Springs Series

Book 1 Tempting His Heart

Book 2 Healing Her Spirit

Book 3 Saving His Soul

Book 4 A Caldwell Wedding

Chosen By Destiny

Book 1 Blayke

Made in the USA
Coppell, TX
19 August 2024

36163150R00059